Rio Bonito

Joe Kettle possessed the grit and fighting blood of his fath
and his father before him. And he needed it, for Wilsh;
Broome – once a loyal foreman of the Standing K ranch – w
using hired gunmen in his effort to seize the Kettle domain.

Supported by an ageing Hector Chaf and Ben McGovrer
Joe sets out to win back his birthright. But each of the thre
men had his own special reason for going up against over
whelming opposition, and it wasn't all to do with property
and livestock.

To overcome Broome's force, they would play a waiting
game, take advantage of the hidden trails and scrub thickets
along the Rio Bonito. Then, when the time was right, they
would not hesitate to meet force with force and guns with
guns.

Rio Bonito

Abe Dancer

A Black Horse Western

ROBERT HALE · LONDON

ISBN 978-0-7090-8767-0

Robert Hale Limited
Clerkenwell House
Clerkenwell Green
London EC1R 0HT

www.halebooks.com

Thank you RMB, and for the use of that name.

Typeset by
Derek Doyle & Associates, Shaw Heath
Printed and bound in Great Britain by
CPI Antony Rowe, Chippenham and Eastbourne

1

The overpowering heat of the New Mexico sun pressed down. It pierced prickly pear and chaparral thickets, made the water simmer in the Rio Bonito. At the eastern end of Hoope Kettle's land, the rays seemed to be concentrating off one corner of the big corral where two boys had been engaged in a ham-fisted, but passionate fist fight.

One, the younger by two years, was the taller by inches, and he had longer arms. His adversary on the other hand was more stockily built. He was by far the strongest, and when his punches landed, they stung the most.

'Your pa would be givin' you a fat ear for comin' home after a scrap like that,' Ben McGovren said with an understanding smile. 'If he ever found out, that is.'

'Judd was spoilin' for a fight. A larrupin' from Pa would be worth it,' Jasper answered back.

'Why *were* you fightin'?' Ben asked.

'He called me a little raggedy-assed foot-soldier. He said I ought to be inside bakin' biscuits.'

Ben nodded. 'It *is* kind o' peculiar not totin' your own saddle, Jasper,' he returned understandingly. 'We ought to see about gettin' you some sort o' cow pony. Meantime, get cleaned up, 'cause your pa's comin'.'

'Them boys o' mine been fightin' again?' Hoope Kettle asked of his 'puncher.

5

'Yeah. I guess young Jasper can only stand so much raggin',' Ben answered. 'But in *that*, he kind o' reminds me o' someone,' he added, after a little thought.

'Seems to me the boy's got a dose o' snake bile in him,' another voice chimed in. It was Wilshaw Broome the foreman who had closed in behind Kettle.

Another of Kettle's cowboys called Hector Chaf, unfolded his long legs. He eased himself down and stood alongside the high pole fence of the corral. 'The snakes around here only anger when you disturb 'em,' he replied. 'An' they rattle before they bite you,'

Broome smiled thinly and shook his head. 'Jasper smacked Judd on the nose. An' that was Judd strikin' back at the funny side of it.'

Ben hopped down from where he'd been sitting beside Hector. 'Judd's been ridin' his little brother for many moons,' he told him. 'I don't reckon he figured on Jasper yet havin' the sand to hit back.'

'It's mostly what young uns do,' Kettle said, good-naturedly. 'It's a way o' gettin' their range. This ain't Philadelphia, ain't even Oklahoma City. There'll be a proper time for 'em to learn etiquettes an' the like.'

'Let's get you lazy roosters goin',' Broome addressed Ben and Hector. 'Get down to the stock, like Mr Kettle wants, or he'll be watchin' *me* kick the bejasus out o' *you* two.'

'Listen, Broome,' Hector snapped back, 'if the boss wants me an' Ben to do somethin', he'll say. We don't rise to your bark, an' we never will.'

Broome cast a sharp glance at Hoope Kettle. But there was no support, and with a dark scowl he started to walk away.

'Hey, Broome,' Hector said quietly, striding after him. 'Are you ridin' into Lemmon tonight?'

The foreman paused and looked doubtfully at the tall

cowboy. 'Why? What's it to you?'

'I'm curious o' the company you been keepin' there,' Hector said. 'Sounds like it might be where you got acquainted with that bile you mentioned.'

Anger distorted Broome's harsh face. He thought of retaliating, but the look of challenge in Hector's eyes checked him. He turned away but Hector continued to bait him.

'I know for some devious reason you've been makin' up to Judd,' he said. 'But neither of 'em are much more'n weaners, so don't go usin' 'em to score points off. An' don't try to divi 'em up. I'm watchin' you real close, mister.'

Close by, Hoope Kettle shook his head as he looked his boys up and down. 'How the both o' you were bred from the same stock, is one o' them marvels o' nature,' he grated. 'I'm thinkin' if I put you both out to pasture, maybe you'll come back more forbearin', not with an outright likin' for each other.'

'Is pasture your way o' sayin' school, Pa?' Jasper asked excitedly.

'It might be *one* way. We'll talk on it at supper,' Kettle said.

That evening, Judd didn't eat with the family. He took a bowl of stew up to his room, stayed there sullen and morose. The only feeling he had for his parents was callow resentment, like he'd held for some time. As a consequence, he missed the talk that decided he'd be leaving the safety of the ranch for some learning years in Gallup. Shortly after that, Hoope Kettle also arranged for Jasper to attend school in Albuquerque for *his* share of an education. One hundred and fifty miles between his constantly squabbling boys was more than adequate, Kettle considered wryly.

Two months later, the big headquarters was a strangely

quiet place after they'd gone, but the stern rancher never let out that he missed them, not even to his wife. Furthermore, the man's loyalty prevented him from admitting that maybe he missed one more than the other.

One day he suggested tellingly to Ben McGovren that a straight saplin' was most likely to make a straight tree.

'Yeah,' Ben replied. 'It'll grow the longest too.'

2

Hoope Kettle, Hector Chaf and Ben McGovren were coasting a low ridge. Keeping back from the summit, only now and again did they catch a glimpse of the country beyond. Hector stood in the stirrups, but even he could see little more than a great blanket of blue New Mexico sky. He pointed eastward, toward the bottom land where the course of Rio Bonito ran.

'There's the draw was tellin' you about, boss.' he said. 'It pulls down to the water between a long stretch o' pear. I don't figure stock woulda drifted that way, unless they was put in at this end.'

'Stock? You seen our stock down there?' Kettle asked.

'Not exactly. But late yesterday they was there,' Hector said, softly.

'How d'you know that?' the rancher continued a little impatiently. 'I know you an' Ben was het up some when you come back from Lemmon last evenin', but I put it down to the liquor. You goin' to tell me it was somethin' else?'

'Yeah, sort of. I know that when somethin' sounds like an' looks like, it probably is.'

Kettle drew his mount to a stop. 'You got some pigtail in you, Hec?' he said sharply. 'What the hell are you tryin' to say?'

Hector's arm took in a great loop of country. 'It was this

section of range that didn't give us anywhere near our tally on the roundup. Then yesterday, Ben an' me seen the Wystan crew. They was way yonder, puttin' together a fair drive herd.'

'Go on,' Kettle encouraged.

'The way that feller's built up over the last two or three years, must be somethin' in his share o' the water. O' course, down there, at the other end o' the narrow draw, there's a ford where the water don't go high enough to wet their bellies.'

Kettle shook his head as if totally bewildered. 'There you go again. Talk some sense for God's sake,' he snapped,

'I seen a white face *this* side; then he appears *that* side. That's what we saw. I reckon he must've used the ford. Then again. . . ?'

Kettle nodded with slow understanding. 'An' then again. . . ?' he echoed.

'Well, I seen one such little un' rompin' round hereabouts. He was wearin' his smart Standin' K brand, an' *now*, stap me if we didn't see the same critter yesterday far side o' the Bonito.'

'So what? It wouldn't be the first young un' to breach its pasture,' Kettle said, and looked towards Ben.

Ben nodded in agreement, 'Yeah, but to pick up a new brand on the way?' he queried.

'Do you two mean what I think you mean?'

'You just need to picture it, boss. If someone was to take no more'n three short burns at the K – two closin' at the front, one closin' at the back – what you got?'

'A goddamn necktie party, *that's* what,' Kettle returned with mounting irritation.

'Yeah, 'cause that *someone's* shaped a Facin' West mark. To our local way o' thinkin' that ain't too far from Yule Wystan's brand.'

10

'You need a bit more goddamn proof than speculation, an' bein' able to recognize the face of a goddamn stray,' Kettle rasped out.

'But it weren't only recognizin' the baby beef,' Hector started to say, 'we got somethin' else.'

'What you mean, *got*?'

Hector twisted round, drew two dotting irons from his saddle boot. Both rods had a short bar on one end. 'We found 'em, boss. Maybe a quarter-mile down the draw. They'd been thrown into the pear.'

With a thoughtful gaze that flicked between Hector and Ben, Kettle took hold of one of the irons. He thought for a moment, then nodded. 'Let me guess,' he said. 'Between 'em they switch my lone K mark to Wystan's, west-facin' arrows, yeah?'

'Yeah, that's right, boss,' Hector answered. 'An' you don't need to be no smart brand burner to work it.'

'Why didn't you show me this before now, Hec?' Kettle asked grimly.

'We wanted to think it out, boss. Then when we did, we wanted you here. Get us a better perspective,' Ben said. 'Give the story some lard, so to speak.'

The three men looked back over the ridge and far beyond. What was evident in their eyes and thoughts didn't bode well for some men along the Rio Bonito.

'How'd you come across them irons an' the route through?' Kettle asked Hector, a few minutes later.

'Mounts rode straight at the pear. We tried to hold 'em back but they went on in,' Hector replied. 'They found a break. We came out east o' the corral. Must've saved us nigh on three miles if we'd taken the draw an' come round.'

'Are you sayin' that someone's workin' an iron this side o' the Bonito?' Kettle eyed his man keenly.

'Yeah. It was kind o' dark, but yeah, that's what we reckon.'

'You told me everythin' now, Hec?'

Hector shook his head. 'Not *everythin'*, boss. You got to leave me *some* stuff,' he said and smiled fleetingly. 'But I *was* talkin to Quedo Lunes last night when we got back. He said somethin' that made me think I ought to get back to him. So maybe later, after chow.'

For a moment, Kettle considered what Hector had said. 'Well, I can't think what that could be. Quedo's a man who don't mix. Sometimes he talks to his friends . . . his *amigos*,' he said.

'Well, he has got somethin' to say, I'll find out.'

Again, Kettle looked thoughtfully at the big 'puncher. 'When do you reckon they'll be drivin' this herd? Soon?'

'They'd have been bedded down near the home pasture last night. If they start with five or six miles today, sundown'll bring 'em close to the water at Lizard Pass. That means they go through at first light.'

'An' how many riders you reckon Wystan's payin'?' Kettle's voice was now turning cool and thoughtful.

'I never reckoned on him goin' over a dozen payroll, but there's maybe twenty or so now. What do *you* reckon, Ben?'

'More. I saw 'em spread out on the flat. Most of 'em were packin' irons . . . rifles too.'

Kettle swore. 'I'll get Broome to set up a bunch o' riders,' he said decisively. 'He can pick them that can handle 'emselves. I'll shell out fightin' wages if I have to.'

'Let's hope he picks those who know what side their corn's buttered,' Hector agreed.

'What do you mean by that, Hec?' Kettle asked of his man. 'Broome is straight enough, ain't he? Are you suggestin' somethin' else I should know about?' he asked.

Hector shrugged. 'I'm just sayin' we ought to be careful

12

who we let in on the reasonin'.'

'Huh, seems all of a sudden I'm learnin' a passel o' new stuff about those in my employ, Hec. But if you reckon you're on to somethin', I'll let *you* pick the men.'

'No, boss. We'll give you their names, but *you* tell 'em. Make sure Owen Pruitt's with 'em. Say we're hazin' out o' the brush. Tell 'em the pear an' chaparral's spread. There's a biggish number lost in the tangle. I'll work up a plan on how best to handle all o' this.'

'Yeah, you do that.' Kettle stopped just short of a smile. 'You never let me down, Hec. Don't go startin' now.'

3

'Goddamn it, Hec,' Hoope Kettle roared towards the beamed ceiling of his ranch-house den. Then he turned to face his top hand. 'While you're swallowin' dust, I'll be settin' out a line o' ropes between the willows either side o' that crossin',' he threatened. 'An' If folk want to see them cow-thieves dancin' a jig, they know where to come.'

'Yes, boss,' Hec responded smartly. 'Meantime, you stay away from Wystan. Remember he's probably hired 'imself a gunny or two if he's stickin' it to our cattle.'

'That's easier said than done, Hec,' Kettle responded thoughtfully. 'But now I've picked your boys, *you* can pound leather. Go get 'em.'

Late that same afternoon, a dozen men rode with Hector Chaf and Ben McGovren. They swept northward in the general direction of the land that Hoope Kettle's father had gifted Ben's father after helping him battle with the Apache. As far as all but three men knew, the land with its broad ring of scrub was their objective. Each man had a Navaho blanket and slicker on his cantle, corn dodgers and a carbine in his saddle pockets. They were mostly young men and a touch reckless. They were picked because they would follow their two top hands through hell and high water, or more realistically, hog-wallow mesquite. Ironically, the same couldn't be said about those who'd side with Hoope Kettle's foreman, Wilshaw Broome.

When Hector had asked for only twelve men, Kettle had objected, said that twenty-five rifles would lay waste to twelve. But that was before he'd fully heard through Hector's plan.

The McGovrens' stump farm homestead was ten miles north of the Standing K land, but a couple of miles short of that, Hector and his men circled to the east, cut the trail that crossed the Rio Bonito before going on to Lemmon. Then they turned north-east, headed into a wide sweep around the path of the drive herd. If the fourteen men were going to reach the far side of Lizard Pass before dawn, they would be riding hard through the night.

It didn't take long for Hector to figure out the Lizard Pass route. Beyond the line of ridges where Lizard Pass cut its course was a broad stretch of open country. At the far end ran one of the main drive trails. To go south-east by way of Lemmon would not only be a longer way, but the herd would be within the scope of a Standing K line rider. Except for pay-day visits to Lemmon, Kettle waddies had little incentive in travelling the country east of Rio Bonito. Long stay 'punchers who'd been with the outfit more than a couple of years had on more than one occasion pursued freelance maverickers across the flats to the Lizard Rim. But Hoope Kettle didn't care much for what went on east of the Rio Bonito, so the river had usually become the limit of their chase. What was happening now though was rustling, and as Ben asided to Hector Chaf, 'Boss is gettin' up more steam than the Santa Fe Flyer.'

So, the south-east trail past Lemmon was out of it according to Hector's reckoning, and the north-east was impassable for anything close to herd size. But that was the course the two 'punchers and their string of doughty riders had to

15

follow. If they took to the flats which extended far in that direction, the drumming of hoofs would carry through the still night air, so they used the short ridges, twisting and turning through arroyos and dry gulches.

In the deep twilight they pegged their mounts and eased the cinches. Around a smokeless fire they boiled coffee, drank it with their dodgers, beef biscuits and hard-boiled eggs. They rolled and smoked a cigarette, then again forked leather along the winding trail. It was open, rough country, but the night light was fair, and before dark, Hector and Ben had set their course with a star to guide them by.

Now and again a stumble thumped the rider into his saddle horn, but the ensuing low curse, created a swell of sniggering and it eased the tension. The Standing K riders now knew the exact nature of the mission, and that daylight would probably bring the confrontation. They also knew that men who play the rustling game prefer the chances of flying lead to the mortal gather of a hangman's rope.

The bright guide star had swung far in its orbit before Hector topped the hogback he'd been aiming for. He rode down the far side to level ground, drew rein while the crew gathered around him. For a moment he looked east, made a thin smile at the first breaking signs of the new day.

'Remember, boys, we don't want no tack jinglin',' he told them. 'We've still got more'n a mile to go, but lookin' at that sky, we'll make it fast. Lizard Pass opens up in a big maw, close to a quarter-mile across before it clears the ridge. When them beeves come through, they'll spread like gravy on a plate.' Hector glanced at Ben, before going on, 'I'll take three o' you to the far side an' work the narrows. Ben'll do the same this side. Between us, we'll see if we can bring down enough critters to stop the run.' He paused again for a moment. 'Where's Owen?' he asked.

Without fuss, a lanky 'puncher worked his mount to

Hector's side.

'Here's your play, Owen,' Hector told him. 'We'll leave you five o' the boys. Set two of 'em for a picket rope. We won't be wastin' time . . . just hop an' run. Three o' you make a line where the maw narrows . . . 'bout a hundred yards across. We'll let two or three o' the point riders through, you keep 'em off our necks. If it works an' we start a back run, just get our horses to us.'

The riders heeled their mounts, chased and beat the purple shades of first light. Without an exchanged word, Ben and three of the men swung down from their saddles, grabbed their carbines and ran for the steep rocky slope of the pass. Another rider gathered the reins of the four horses and raced them back, staked them behind the outcrop of a boulder ridge. Moments later, Hector and his men were doing the same on the other side of the gaping cut, racing Ben and his men to their comparative positions.

Hector posted his three, called quietly for them to wait. 'Do nothin' until me or Ben start the big carouse,' he told them. 'I'm goin' to drop down the other side o' the ridge, just low enough for 'em not to sight me against that brightenin' sky,' he explained,

Five minutes later, Hector cleared the ridge, and tucked himself in below the skyline. Five more minutes and he sniffed the air, picked up the rising spread of sound that all cowmen recognized.

4

The deep purple sky was changing rapidly. Fingers of blue, pink and grey were streaking from the east. But to the west, Hector picked out a flickering light, and he knew that the Facing West range cook was setting up breakfast. A little later from somewhere on the flat, a long bellow addressed the brightening sky. It was answered from another point, taken up by another then another. It gave Hector a chance to figure the main gather and breadth of the herd, the direction it was likely to head after moving out.

But a moment later he stopped his measurement and froze. He held his breath, tried desperately not to shake as two rattlesnakes slithered sinuously side-by-side across his outstretched left leg. He cursed, wondered whether he'd disturbed them. I've gone an' bedded down with a couple o' goddamn courtin' side-winders, he cursed again, inwardly. He lay very still, waited a long minute for any warning rattle. Then he shuddered, shifted his position and cursed again, as he realized he'd made coldharbour camp where the ridge rock gained its warmth from the approaching day.

He turned his head towards the far side of the pass and grinned. 'I was tellin' someone the other day that buzzworms only strike if you disturb or provoke 'em. An' you'll probably be back this way later in the day,' he said, and wondered if Ben MeGovren was having any better luck.

The light grew and Hector examined his surroundings, looked for better cover. He decided that his refuge was as good as anywhere else. 'We can't all be wrong,' he muttered, looking suspiciously around him. He swung his attention back to the flats, to the waking cattle. The night riders would be in and the point would be shaping up. Soon, less than a half mile distant, the herd began to move.

Hector knew that swing riders would take their positions in front of the flankers. They'd shape a bottleneck for the pass, to squeeze the herd through. They'd also be the riders who'd make it scratchy for Ben and himself, once the fight kicked off. He had another look at the short sloping ridge before him, estimated the angles from which it would give him protection from rustlers' bullets.

The broad dark shadow rolled towards Hector's cover. The ground picked up the low rumbling tremor as thousands of hoofs took up their day's march. Far back, a dust curtain rose, hung suspended in the air. Later it would swirl and billow into choking clouds when the breeze picked up.

Hector spat dryness, loosened his pistol in its holster and pulled the Sharps carbine towards him. The lead steers were coming into sight now, and the air was filled with yips and yells, the crack of whips, the dull click of horns. The sound of approaching hoofs grew into a heavy grumble, and Hector made out the riders on point. He expected three, maybe four riders, but when they were a hundred yards distant, he counted up to a dozen. He began cursing again, hoped that Owen Pruitt and his men weren't in new, increased danger. In their favour was the fact that Yule

19

Wystan's riders had no inkling of who and what was lying in wait for them at the pass, but there was enough of them to kick out fast and resolute once they'd cleared the narrows.

Hector was in no position or frame of mind to change his strategy for the engagement. They must all of them take their chances. But he reflected that once the cattle were into the pass, Hoope Kettle would at least have fewer guns throwing lead at him.

It was an hour earlier in the first light of dawn that Hoope Kettle sent his big bay splashing through the ford. A single line of fourteen horsemen followed him through the water, made it up the bank close to the tunnel through the prickly pear. Six miles of flat stretched before them, six miles to Lizard Pass, maybe four, to where the big herd would be milling.

Hoope Kettle wasn't a man who'd spent his life out-tolerating everyone. But he'd always wanted to be certain of a man's guilt before seeing him brought to justice, let alone hanged. By the same token, he'd never doubted Hector Chaf, never questioned the man's judgement. But now it was personal and the rancher wanted to get involved, sense the wrong. He wanted to mete out the anger he carried, and he didn't want to wait long.

Up ahead rode the man who'd worked Kettle's Standing K brand into the Facing West brand. Such tricks – using a running iron ahead of the roundup – had been done many times before, but the last time Yule Wystan had tried it, it was a hurried botched job, and he'd had to scuttle from south of the Black Mesa in Arizona. But this time he'd worked long and patiently to make this a winning re-brand. And he'd managed to stay low, because he wanted it to be his final move. He'd built a crew of thirty on his payroll, but he considered it a worthy investment. Of the great herd he was now driving, barely a third carried a genuine Facing

West brand – a contrived brand, solely for the purpose of rustling.

Wystan was riding drag with half-a-dozen trigger men strung out to his left and right. With the bulk of the herd moving, the rest needed little prodding, and Wystan had detailed the hired guns to ride with him. The men rode with added early morning frostiness because they had spent the night time hours guarding against what might come at them from across the shallows of the Rio Bonito.

But one man sided up to Wystan with a relieved smirk on his face. 'I'm sure glad we're movin', Mr Wystan,' he said.

'Yeah, so am I. But it's only when we're across the water an' through the pass, no one can touch us.'.

'If you're still worryin' about that brace o' K men we spotted yesterday, there was nothin' for 'em to get suspicious about. They didn't see nothin.'

The light was getting stronger, and Wystan looked behind, and then all around him. 'That's a nothin' you don't know for certain,' he said. 'I got me a belly gnaw, Ringo. It's the belief that if somethin' can go wrong it probably will. An' it's *when* that's got me rattled, I don't mind admittin'.'

'The only feelin in your belly's probably from eatin' cow dust,' Ringo Chawke countered. 'You're back here fillin' up with alkali. Why not ride out to the flank? From there you'll see the pass real good.'

'What's that?' Wystan demanded sharply and twisted in his saddle. 'What's that?' he repeated. 'You hear it?'

'Hell, you sure are rattled,' Ringo answered, without taking the trouble to look or listen.

Wystan faced backward, one hand gripping the cantle. 'You can hear *that*, can't you?' he growled.

'Yeah, somethin' maybe,' Ringo said quietly. 'But I can't see nothin'.'

21

'Ride to the near flank,' Wystan told him. 'Call in the men that side. Send Cruz out to the other flank. It might *be* nothin', but I ain't takin' any chances. An' nor's my scrawny ol' neck.'

5

Wystan was still twisting around in his saddle when Kettle's bay pounded through the early morning gloom. He'd been nervy, not ready to be taken off his guard, and within a few of the approaching horse's big strides, he'd set himself to strike back. He wanted away from the Rio Bonito country, had made up his mind to shoot his way out if he had to. But he knew his men were coming from either flank and, knowing their professional abilities, he didn't feel that insecure.

'You got some sort o' burr under your blanket?' Wystan rumbled, used a tight smile to disguise the movement of his gun hand at the sudden confrontation.

'Yeah, somethin' like that,' Kettle clipped back, knowing full well he had the advantage of surprise. 'I've rode out here to return somethin'.'

The pair of running irons sailed through the air towards Wystan and he threw up an arm as a defending response.

'What the hell are those?' he yelled, realizing he'd been caught. He saw that Kettle's hand rested on the butt of his Colt.

'Keep very still, Wystan,' Kettle threatened. 'Make a move for that ol' hog leg an' I'll just have to do what I got to do, without hearin' your explanation.'

'I ain't got time for nonsense jawbonin' with you, Kettle,' Wystan snarled. 'I got me a trail herd to run.'

Wystan's men were now closing in. The man was thinking to hold Kettle up, keep his attention while their guns took him out. That's what he was paying them fighting wages for. But then Wystan saw a few, well-armed Standing K men riding towards their own boss. Providing cover, more men had carbines with barrels lowered against their horses flanks. Wystan's men had taken notice too, wondered whether they should have broken cover so soon.

'So you ain't got time to explain these irons, eh?' Kettle said. 'That's a shame, but not a problem, 'cause the herd ain't runnin' anywhere until I've had me a closer look at 'em. Meantime, I suggest you an' your friends draw off a piece.'

'You're as close to my steers as you're goin' to get,' Wystan yelled. He wondered why his men's pistols hadn't started barking on either side of him. 'Goddamnit,' he swore; they all knew what they'd been hired for. He glanced to left and right, saw their stillness in the saddle. There was something wrong and he didn't know what it was. 'Goddamnit,' he swore again directly at Kettle. 'What the hell are you doin' out here?'

'Takin' a look at my steers you're thinkin' o' runnin' off,' Kettle gritted.

Wystan was instantly taken aback. Before he could think of a way to counter the outburst, Kettle was off again.

'I know what's been dotted with those irons. You burned a new brand onto my Standin' K,' Kettle charged. 'But I ain't a vindictive man, an' most o' the time I think the best o' most everyone. It's because I don't normally take stuff that ain't mine, I'll be content with cuttin' out them steers that are. What you do next's up to you, but I wouldn't do anythin' else stupid, 'cause so far into this new day you been real lucky.'

Wystan had regained a degree of composure after discov-

24

ering the identity of his challenger. 'Listen, Kettle,' he snarled back, 'I appreciate your sense o' justice, but shortly there'll be upwards o' thirty o' my riders chargin' in here, an' they ain't in the mood for an "excuse me". For me, this ain't personal, but they ain't goin' to see it that way.'

For all his hot-headedness, Hoope Kettle retained a thought for his men. He was waiting for the moment when, using surprise, they could match the speed of Wystan's gunslingers. Besides, he remembered it was Hector Chaf or Ben McGovren that would start their big carouse. If *he* kicked off with any rash gunplay, it could wreck their best laid plans. So he grinned weakly, watched Wystan's hand dropping imperceptibly lower.

'That's the trouble, I do see this sort o' thing as personal,' he returned, shaking his head. 'An' it just don't seem fair,' he added, continuing the weak grin at Wystan. But he was stalling, holding out for as long as he could, acting the loser.

'Yeah, life's a bitch, ain't it?' Wystan quipped. 'We got the drop, an' there ain't a goddamn thing you can do about it. The point's well through the pass now, an' nothin' could stop the rest from followin'.'

A moment later, the sharp report of a carbine cracked down from the pass. It was what Kettle 'punchers needed, and most of them responded.

Wystan jerked at the report, but managed to flash a hand to his gun, But Kettle had already fired, and his bullet smashed into the meat of Wystan's right shoulder. He rowelled deep and the big bay closed the distance between the two men in little more than a single leap. Kettle pushed his Colt back into its holster, and grabbed for Wystan's coat front. With his other hand he pulled his lariat off the saddle horn and flipped a loop around Wystan's flagging body.

A bullet chewed across the flesh of Kettle's lower arm.

The man turned, but he only saw Ringo Chawke catch a bullet high in his chest. Wystan's man made no sound, just crashed from the saddle, was dead before hitting the hard-packed dirt. Kettle swung back to his wounded prisoner, called for one of his riders to take the nervy horse's reins.

'Keep an eye on this goddamn cow thief,' he rasped. 'He'll probably try an' die on you, rather than face what's comin' to him. Get him to the Bonito, an' wait there for me.'

Kettle pulled his Colt, again, confronted the ongoing fight. 'Jeesus,' he cursed out loud, 'I'm a bear's ass if this ain't personal. They're *my* goddamn steers.'

Most of the men who'd joined the Wystan payroll were considering the situation, the likely outcome. They were on fighting wages, but guarding the herd and running steers wasn't quite the same as a chancy, hard-hosed gunfight.

Kettle sensed the dilemma. He looked around him with rising confidence, but rifles opened up from both flanks. At the crash of gunfire, the approaching cattle recoiled from the conflict. They jammed those ahead, created a roil behind them. Around the flanks, the frightened cattle had broken away from the main bunch, were running bug-eyed back across the flats. More followed on until the main herd was streaming that way. The rustlers were quick to take advantage of the running cover, and their fire became unpredictable and volatile, too dangerous for the Standing K men who were milling in a group.

Kettle made a quick assessment of the situation and decided to head for the right flank. He yelled at his men to follow and rowelled the bay. They let off a furious barrage of gunfire as they rode, but the rustlers were bulldogging, cutting between the irritated steers. Any lethal aiming was impossible, and it wasn't long before the rustlers broke and hightailed it towards the ridge. Once there, they would regroup, head to the point of the nearest flank. Kettle yelled again and, as his men pounded into the chase, he waved an arm for them to spread out.

The day's early breezes strengthened, and as the sun rose higher, dust clouds started to blow clear across that flank. Now, Kettle and his men could see all the way to the ridge. A group of Wystan's men was running ahead, back firing as they went. Beyond them, a half-dozen more drew their rifles and prepared to give as good as they were getting. Kettle thought a couple of his men were missing but, quickly evaluating the mood of most others, he decided to continue with the attack. He hadn't forgotten Wystan's men out on the far flank, expecting that very soon they would round the herd. If they did, they would sweep around to the rear, where the Standing K men would be trapped, caught between two waves of gunfire.

Up ahead of the advancing riders, gunfire cracked, echoed along the walls of the Pass. Realizing it was one of Wystan's men who had set off the fight, Owen Pruitt had quickly placed his men. For his own position, he chose what seemed a likely outcrop, but in the turmoil had misjudged its potential for cover. He watched Wystan's point riders come through and thought he'd be overrun by their number. He cursed, for a long moment considered riding back to find proper cover. But Hector expected him to stay, so stay he would.

6

The first riders came on six abreast. Six more straggled back to the lead steers, where Owen Pruitt could plainly see the violent tossing and brandishing of horns. They advanced to within a hundred yards, then the line separated. Three rode to each side, formed a line for the cattle as those behind pushed up. Pruitt was ready, anxious to open up with his carbine, but he waited for Hector or Ben to give the signal. As he took stock, his head and shoulders silhouetted against the lightening skyline. To his right, he saw a rider throw up his rifle, felt the snatch as the bullet ripped across his shoulder blades, and he cursed loudly.

The other riders jerked guns from their saddle holsters, but two were shot down almost immediately. From four or five directions, rifles started to bark and blaze. Those men bringing up the rear whirled their mounts, dashed back the way they had come. But they found the pass was jammed with cattle that were being felled by a murderous barrage of gunfire from either bank. Trapped, the nine men realized they had to throw up a fight before making a run for the open country. They kicked spurs, as from behind them more rifles opened up. Horses went down, and the riders fought from behind the stricken mounts. For some time, the battle between the cattlemen continued with unabated fervour.

Like his partner, Ben McGovren had been looking things over when it got somewhere near the first light. From his side of the pass, he saw the unusually large number of point riders coming on with the cattle following close. Ben also saw a dozen more riders along the flank before him. They were going to station themselves where the ridge dipped back to a false opening, attempt to keep the cattle from jamming into a mill. That would create real trouble for the bulk of the herd. On consideration, Ben thought it best to leave the cattle plugging to his men and Hector's crew. So, he sniffed a suitable curse, took resolute aim with his carbine and began the alternative work.

He was surprised when a riderless horse went galloping by, and in attempting to recognize the mount, he caught a bullet on the crown of his shoulder. More gunfire cut down his return of fire, and in his ducking in and out of cover, another bullet sliced across the side of his neck.

'Goddamn all you brand burners,' he cursed loudly. 'I'll run out o' lives before bullets,' he added, knowing that he'd received a good fighting ration from Hoope Kettle.

Ben pumped out another salvo, but there was no luxury of knowing the effect he was having. Minutes later, he was reloading when the lead exchange stuttered, then stopped. He waited a moment before risking a look, but when he did, he saw the Wystan gunmen streaking towards the tail of the distant herd. From there, he could still hear firing, and he could see the herd was starting to turn, But then his interest returned to the Pass, where he knew Hector should be. In between breaks in the dust clouds, he saw his friend and his jaw dropped. He blinked and shook his head clear, for Hector's behaviour at that moment wasn't what he expected. The tall 'puncher was on his feet, standing with no apparent fear of presenting himself as a target.

'He's read too many o' them dime-store novels,' Ben

29

rasped. 'He thinks he's at the Little Big Horn.'

But Hector wasn't shooting at the cattle or the rustlers. He had the barrel of his carbine lowered, was shooting around his own feet.

Ben was utterly amazed. 'What the hell you shootin' at?' he yelled out, as Hector continued to pump bullets into the dirt.

Now the firing around the pass had almost stopped, but the bawling of cattle and a ripple of gunfire on Hector's side of the big herd was still making some noise.

'You lumberin' fool,' he yelled, a grasp of the situation spreading across his face. 'Get yourself out o' there.'

Hector give a quick glance around him and spat a few garbled words. He hopped a step backwards, then broke into a run towards the flats.

Ben watched for a moment, then saw that nearer to him, the cattle had started to mill, were headed into a certain stampede. Before disappearing into another swell of dust, he saw the chuck-wagon driver wheel his mule team, lash them into an anxious run. Where Hector was heading, a steady hail of gunfire was closing on the ridge.

Ben waited no longer, He ran from his cover; within moments resumed a stream of agitated curses as he leapt over fallen steers. He gained the other side to see that Hector was now down on one knee shoving cartridges into his magazine. Hector saw him coming, waved an arm out towards the flats where a bunch of riders were backing up. Beyond them, and closing fast, Hoope Kettle was leading a string of his men straight at the Wystan guns.

Hector nodded and Ben understood the meaning. He heard the click of Hector's breech block, another as he levered. He grimaced at the soreness that spread across his shoulders and neck, but he put up his own carbine. Both men pulled their triggers almost simultaneously and one rider went down, another crumpled forward in the saddle. They jerked up fresh cartridges, paused in determined aim, and another man fell from his horse. The remaining Wystan riders saw the devastating collapse of their companions. Most of them would prefer the odds of being hit by lead, to the summary justice of a neck-tie party. But now they were surrounded and defeated, and they opted for the chancer's employ of uncertainty. To a man, they dropped their weapons and raised their arms.

Within moments, Kettle and his men were winding lariats around them, jerking them secure in their saddles. Their horses were strung out in a line and Kettle was considering a detail of two riders to lead them to the Rio Bonito, where he'd earlier dispatched Yule Wystan.

'I'll wager they ain't got much of a future,' Hector predicted dourly.

From where the Standing K men sat their mounts, a great dust cloud was billowing slowly into the north-west. They could still see heaving rumps and high raised tails, but the whole herd had turned, was now in full run. It had taken a whole day to cover that six-mile stretch, but now it looked as if they would be back at where they started in a matter of minutes. The men knew that if the animals hit the creek at that speed, the pile up would cost many more deaths.

'How are things up front, Hec?' Hoope Kettle asked, being mindful of something else.

'They'll be quietenin' down,' Hector answered, as if he knew it.

'Are you hurt?' The rancher took a closer look at his 'puncher.

'No, just bruised up a bit. I was lucky, but for a pinch o' flesh.'

'Hmm. Well, how about the riders on the left flank? Do

you know how many rustlers they took out?'

'I ain't been much involved with takin' out rustlers,' Hector responded. He was still frustrated at not being able to get himself involved. 'I just had a nest o' rattlers gettin' irate at the thought o' me sharin' their nest. ain't got me a horse yet, neither,' he added testily.

'Looked to me like you was stormin' the puncheons on a Friday night,' Ben McGovren laughed.

Kettle shook his head at not fully understanding what Ben was alluding to. He wheeled his bay to look back from where he'd come.

'They ought to be showin' up right soon,' he growled, shoving in fresh cartridges. 'Wystan called that goddamn army o' his in from both sides.'

Hector nodded thoughtfully. Then he pointed to where the herd was moving across the flats like the shadow from a cloud. 'Ain't no chance o' them jiggers comin' round behind you now, boss. If there's any riders still yonder, me an' Ben'll sweep 'em up. We'll chase 'em clear to the border, if we have to.'

'That's right, boss,' Ben agreed. 'Meantime, you got to head off them runnin' steers. Get 'em turned, lest you want 'em bloatin' an' floatin'.'

Kettle spat drily. 'Nice turn o' phrase, Ben,' he gruffed. Then he sat his bay quietly and listened to the new-found silence. A full minute later he pointed forward. Two of his men shifted the prisoners into a line and followed on at a lesser pace.

Not long after, Hector jabbed Ben in the ribs, nodded to where a bloodied Owen Pruitt was bringing in the mounts. The two men quickly looked them over, selected their own as the most suitable for their proposed pursuit of the Wystan riders.

Those remaining of Wystan's rustlers were trapped by the stampeded cattle. They couldn't escape to the south and east, and had the Standing K men before them on the west. They sought to cross the Rio Bonito for an escape, to take their chances through the pear thickets. But Hector and Ben had discussed just such a possibility. They took Kettle's route across the ford and met up with a group of 'puncher's who had been told to string out along the eastern bank.

The desperate rustlers, deeply fearing what awaited them on capture, ran pell-mell into the Standing K sixguns and carbines. They were in disarray, had lost heart for someone else's fight and two more of them fell gravely wounded. To their right and to the north was the rocky, waterless stretch of country, where Hector and Ben had skirted the previous night. As a last chance, the beleaguered men turned back on their tracks, made towards Lizard Pass Ridge. But midway between the Bonito and the ridge, on the northern edge of the flats, Hector and Ben had regrouped with their feisty crew. From behind scattered boulders, the shelter of cracks and fissures in the ravine, they hurled more lead into the skirmish. But their anger had ebbed, and they used the force of their surprise to send the few remaining men scuttling across the ridge, into the water scrape beyond.

'I'd wager a week's pay, not one o' them turkeys stops to take a leak before they reach Chaco Canyon,' Ben drawled tiredly.

It was edging into first dark when Hector and Ben led their remaining force to the crossing. As they approached the bank, skirting the ford, Hector swore profusely and pointed ahead.

'There's the work of a man who likes to be *just* when it comes to sentencin',' he commented.

Ben looked ahead, gasped in fearful awe at the men who

hung from the ends of ropes. The willows bent their pliant branches, the lifeless bodies swayed in the warm breeze.

'Boss said he'd set out a line o' ropes, an' he has,' Ben recalled. 'I'd sort o' forgot all about that. I guess the law's got more important things to do than go chasin' cow thieves.'

'In this neck o' the woods, *Hoope Kettle's* the law. For what they did, these fellers knew the price o' gettin' caught.'

'Yeah,' Ben agreed. 'Probably got dollars in their pants to prove it.'

'Still, it's some price to pay for runnin' off cows.'

The two weary cowboys sat their horses for a while longer, solemnly discussed the outcome of their day.

'Did you see if Wystan was there?' Hec asked his long-time friend.

'Dunno. Difficult to put a name to the state o' *them* faces. Old Hoope's got some hard bark on him, Hec.'

'He's had to have. This land weren't no Garden of Eden, when he first came. The times are changin', but he ain't. Let's hope Jasper an' Judd never see this side o' their pa's disposition.'

'Hmm,' For a moment, Ben thought Hector's remarks over. 'You still thinkin' it was someone on Standin' K payroll who was helpin' the Wystan spread?' he asked.

'I'm snappin' hard at Wilshaw Broome's shadow, Ben, but there's no way o' provin' it. For now, let's keep them thoughts to ourselves. In the boss's present frame of mind, even a notion's as good as a guilty stamp. Besides, there's a couple o' *vaqueros* that Quedo warned me about. I'll see 'em when we get back. They just might have a tale to tell.'

But Hoope Kettle was a keen appraiser of men's short-comings as well as their virtues, and he was back in his ranch-house den some time before Hector and Ben returned.

He called in Quedo Lunes, because he too now wanted information on the allegiance of his crew.

'I'm no protector o' cattle rustlers, *jefe*,' the Mexican wrangler offered at Kettle's request for information. 'You tell me, an' I get it seen to.'

Kettle thanked his loyal wrangler, knew it would be the man's friends who would be taking care of the situation. Whatever happened, the treacherous 'punchers would never be seen on Standing K land again, dead or alive.

Moreover, and a full day prior to that, Hector had advised his boss not to make Wilshaw Broome aware of their plan to chase down Wystan and the Facing West outfit. Instead, he'd persuaded Kettle to send the foreman to Fort Wingate with the ranch's stock wagon. It would mean an overnight stay, but with the spicy attractions of a big town, it wasn't a chore that Broome would likely object to.

Broome returned before full dark the following evening. But later the same night, when excited 'punchers told of the Rio Bonito incident, he responded with an intriguing mix of both outrage and alarm. He sought out Hoope Kettle with the argument that he was ranch foreman, should have been the one to lead any assault on cattle rustlers.

But the ranch boss told him they'd had no time, they'd responded to the shock discovery that the herd was being gathered for a stampede across the Rio Bonito. He suggested that if Broome wanted a fuller explanation he'd best talk to Hector and Ben who had led the fight.

Broome did, with the purpose of intimidating the two waddies. But the foreman got short shrift. Instead, he was put in no doubt as to the price he might eventually have to pay.

Hector Chaf *was* right about times changing. Hoope Kettle had, by virtue of a last hurrah, put an end to large-scale rustling. He'd lost a few men in doing it, but most acknowledged it was an unavoidable outcome. The gunslingers and rustlers whom Hector and Ben had chased from the county wouldn't be reforming, or spreading word of easy money from a rebranding job. The grim tokens that were strung along the banks of the Rio Bonito threw up an unsightly curtain for anyone with lingering doubts.

'Certainly puts me off any crooked doin's,' Ben had said, with matter-of-fact sentiment.

7

As the months, then years passed, there remained a chilly impasse between Hector Chaf and Ben McGovren and the Standing K foreman. But for a reason that maybe only Wilshaw Broome himself could explain, there was never a time when any of them pushed for a face-off.

Jasper and Judd returned from across the state where they had received their schooling. They were no longer boys, but able, strapping young men. As Hector and Ben had foreseen, that to which their father had turned a blind eye, the character traits in each of the youngsters, hadn't changed, just strengthened with time. Judd was surly and wretched, decided to chum up with Wilshaw Broome, rather than have much to do with his father or brother. Jasper on the other side was a cheerful, open young man, bore a likeness to his father and grandfather before him.

Kettle was loyal to both his sons, impartial when it came to any outward show of parental care. However, the elderly rancher did believe in the convention of eldest son being first in line, and consequently detailed more duties to Judd in the way of ranch management. Despite his pleasant demeanour, it didn't take long for Jasper to become frustrated and restless. But for Wilshaw Broome it was a time for which he had long waited. In anticipation of the benefits, he started to throw his weight around once again. For

Hector and Ben it explained a lot, presaged the trouble that would once again run a dark shadow across the land of Standing K.

A new arrival in town was Beth Shortcorn from Hackberry, Arizona. She thought that Lemmon was far enough east to find a less wild society. Jasper thought that funny, made her even more to his liking. Judd also had been an admirer, but Beth was quick to appreciate the difference between the brothers. Favouring Jasper meant there was little chance for someone of Judd's disposition. Jasper was won over and, with his parents' blessing, asked for Beth's hand. The couple were married the same fall, made their home not more than ten miles from the Standing K's home pasture.

About the same time Ben McGovren took a wife. Her name was Aileen, and she too was an incomer up from Las Cruces. They decided to rebuild the tumbledown homestead of Ben's early youth, clear out the pear and matchweed. But nothing much changed for Hector Chaf. Most evenings he rode out to the breeding range to watch the bulls, or strolled to the corral to run an eye over a new breed mare. It was while looking over a fine sorrel one evening with Hoope Kettle that his old friend lost his balance and fell back from a top rail. He landed badly and, because of his stiff bulk, he suffered internal injuries that wouldn't allow him to walk or ride far, ever again.

Either from old-fashioned loyalty, or just plain stubbornness, Kettle continued with Wilshaw Broome as his foreman. But with Judd's growing involvement, it was more in name only, and why Hector never questioned Hoope's decision. But in time, Broome managed to drive a wedge between Judd and his brother. Although sadly aware of Jasper's situation, Hector accepted it as a family matter, that Kettle blood was thicker than water. But in his own way,

Hector could be just as dogmatic as his boss, and he was going to stay close and vigilant until the peace broke. And he'd a grain of an idea just how long that would be.

Gradually, Wilshaw Broome elbowed out any rider whom he suspected of not being too loyal to him and his association with Judd. He reasoned, shrewdly, that if needs be, they'd probably side with Jasper and Hector Chaf – something along the lines of your enemy's enemies are *your* friends. As a consequence of this workforce cull, Hector had no more than three genuine, trusty friends including Jasper, whom Broome couldn't influence or dispose of. Ben McGovren would still side with Hector, and for the least of causes. And there was the bone-handled .44 Colt that was close to Hector's side, day and night. It made up a quartet that grimly satisfied Hector, something for Broome and his cohorts to disregard ever at their peril.

In due time, Beth Kettle gave birth to a husky young son who thrived under the full name of Bruno Joseph Kettle. Then inevitably, but somewhat later, Ben and Aileen produced a daughter.

In one of the outlying adobes that Hoope Kettle had set aside for the married workers, another girl was reaching early womanhood. Her parents were Mexican, her father was the wrangler, Quedo Lunes. Home for mother and daughter was at the furthest section from the main house, no more than five miles from the burgeoning outskirts of Lemmon. One reason this little family had moved that much nearer to town was the intimidating attitude of both Judd and Wilshaw Broome towards Mexican employees and their families.

But despite the flawed circumstances of their housing, Quedo knew that young Clemente was beginning to attract the attention of both these men. There was nowhere more convenient where Quedo could find suitable work, even if he wanted it. So, like Hector Chaf, he accepted his lot tolerantly. His wife did washing and mending for the payroll 'punchers, and Clemente grew ever more attractive as time passed.

The Lunes looked upon Hector as a good and reliable friend, and he was a regular caller at their home when he rode to Lemmon. He'd usually leave it for a Sunday call, when he knew Quedo would be there. After each visit, Clemente would invariably find an extra fund to supplement the family food cupboard, but Hector's calls were becoming less frequent. He'd set himself to keep a closer eye on the Standing K ranch house, where old Hoope's health had started to deteriorate rapidly.

'There's not much any of us can do, Hec,' Jasper said one day. 'He's bein' fed like a weaner calf.'

8

One day, Wilshaw Broome decided to make a courtesy call at the Lunes' adobe. Bearing in mind the man's hostility towards Mexicans, it was a surprising visit, even more so, if the rumours were true that he kept a wife and boy child in a small border town west of Gallup. 'OK for the washin' an' keepin' a friendly cot, but not for the marryin' of,' was his oft quoted opinion of any girl from south of the border.

Clemente and her mother made no mention of the visit to Quedo. At that time, the Standing K foreman hadn't actually said or done anything that could be taken as offensive or unsociable, even. Clemente did mention it to Hector, but he had no idea either, only that the man's intentions were hardly ever principled. Some time later, he recalled Quedo once wistfully told him that because of her striking looks, his daughter would be safer in a Salt Lake seminary.

A month or so on, and Hector saw Broome and Judd roughhousing against one of the Standing K corrals. The pushing and shoving wasn't serious, and obviously at the expense of a third party. They were bragging, claiming as to who would be falling to whom.

'You ridin' the old mare?' Judd said, and sniggered.

'They says to put a *young* trooper on an *old* horse, Judd,' Broome returned with a vulgar laugh.

Hector, not knowing the direction of their crudeness,

shook his head and turned away. Later in the evening, he rode to Lemmon on one of his now even rarer visits. For some fateful reason he didn't feel much like drinking, no more than settling the dust from the ride. He wanted to see Clemente and her ma, thought he'd pay his sober respects on the return to Standing K. He made his way to one of the town's dog-hole saloons, but checked himself before entering. Through the quartered front window, a circle had been smeared through some of the dust layers, and through it he saw Broome and Judd at the end of the bar. Within a few feet stood a gun-toting pair of supporters who had recently taken to riding close to the two men. Hector would have preferred his usual company of sidewinders to any one of that group, and he crossed the dirt-packed street to an even less respectable cantina. He sipped uneasily at a glass of beer, pondered on the unfolding events in and out of the Standing K.

'Don't see much o' you in here,' the barman said after a minute or so.

'You won't see much more, if it's conversation you're lookin' for,' Hector snapped testily.

Untroubled, the barman shrugged. 'No need to kick,' he said. 'I only mentioned it 'cause a little while back, feller came in and had a word with my other customer. I think he said he was lookin' for you.'

'Who was he, this feller?'

'Hard to tell under one o' them big sombreros.'

'You sayin' he was Mexican?'

'Yeah, an' he seemed genuinely wound up. Then again, these chillis are always pretty excited about somethin',' he added with a boorish sneer.

'Aren't they just,' Hector said more to himself than the barman who had already turned away. He sucked at the last of his beer. 'It must've been Quedo. An' he'd only come

42

lookin' for me if there was some sort of trouble,' he added. 'This other customer o' yours – I don't suppose you'd know where he'd have gone?' he called out to the barman.

The barman shook his head, and Hector returned a thin smile. 'No, I didn't think so,' he said, and quickly left the bar. Outside, he heeled his claybank mare in the flanks, turned its head for the end of town.

'Goddamn, I knew it . . . could feel it,' he rasped, and kicked on through the darkness, rode hard into the few miles that would take him to the Lunes' adobe. He saw no sign of any other riders, and within fifteen minutes he was dragging the mare into a sliding stop.

'Where the hell are you?' he called out. 'Where's your goddamn lights?' He swung from the saddle, ran fearfully for the front door.

Knowing it was pointless, he didn't knock, pushed the door wide and peered into the pitch-dark interior. He stepped inside, struck a match and held it at arm's length until it burned. He didn't feel the pain as he extinguished the burnt splinter between his fingertips. He cursed, leaned against the edge of the door, lit another match and cursed again. Then he moved forward and lit the tallow lamp that stood in the middle of the scoured oak table.

The yellow light spread to reveal Clemente and her mother sprawled on the puncheon floor. They had both been shot dead, blood had run thick and viscous from their upper bodies. Clemente was clutching a knife. She had died either wanting to protect herself or her mother, probably both.

Beside her mother – Quedo's wife – Hector then saw the second knife, but its blade was still glistening wet. Hector gritted his teeth, groaned when he noticed the blood across her neck, a dark ribbon that had trickled from where part of her ear had been snatched away. 'They gone an' tagged you,' he muttered thick and hoarse. 'I reckon you both must've give somethin' in return, for 'em to do that.'

He took both knives and placed them on the table. 'I'll get you taken care of,' he said absent-mindedly. 'I'll do it for all of us.' For some long minutes, he stood sentinel in the darkness, unsure of when, what moment to make a move.

'I was hopin' that some sort o' law had paid Lemmon a visit, but it ain't,' he muttered eventually. Then he walked from the room, stepped carefully so as not to jingle his spurs. Outside, he tugged gently at the mane of his horse. 'They're your family, Quedo. Why ain't you here, lookin after 'em?' he asked of no one.

He wondered about Quedo's whereabouts for a brief moment, then undid the flap of his a saddle pouch. From deep down he drew out a big, ancient pepperbox pistol. 'Looks like you an' me finally got a job, ol' feller,' he said quietly.

9

Hector tied his mare at the hitching post, walked calmly up the steps to the single door of the saloon. He had a quick look through the window, saw Wilshaw Broome's hired guns were now seated, and playing Slippery Sam. There were a few drifters and 'punchers standing at the bar, but none of them was recognizable as trouble for him.

It was obvious from the mannerisms of the card players that they had both consumed a fair amount of liquor. It was very late now, and Hector knew that the men had been at it for a few hours. Suits me, he thought. The more drunk *you* get, the more sober *I* get.

He quickly went through the door and within three or four paces was standing very close to the card table.

'I'm lookin' for Wilshaw Broome an' Judd Kettle,' he told the man who had raised his boozy eyes to him.

'They've been gone a couple of hours,' the man answered, and threw a quick glance at his partner who had dealt him another card.

Hector didn't know that Wilshaw Broome had told the gunmen to say exactly that, and only a quarter-hour earlier, when they'd seen him on the outskirts of town arriving from the direction of the Lunes' adobe. And he didn't know that they had their orders not to let him leave town alive. The men didn't know the reason, and they weren't paid to care

45

or ask questions.

'Oh, I know just about how long they've been gone,' Hector said. 'I meant, I was lookin' for 'em. So, do you know where I can find 'em?'

'Back at the bunk house by now, I should think.'

'You an' your friend been here all evenin'?' Hector asked him.

'Yeah, if it's any o' your business, Mr Chaf,' the man smiled knowingly. 'Ol' Broome spoke o' you,' he suggested, eyeing Hector's holstered Colt.

'I'm sure he did,' Hector responded without a smile. 'But other than takin' his fightin' pay, don't pretend it's *your* business either. You ain't much good to man nor beast sittin' here playin' the papers an' swallowin' forty-rod.'

'If you got somethin' in mind, feller, you're a mite outnumbered,' the man tested.

'Yeah, *maybe*. But what you an' the dealer here's got to ask yourselves *is*, what happens if all seven o' these here barrels go off at once?' Hector threatened. With that, he took a step back and drew his hand from inside the front of his jacket. He smiled icily as he levelled the old multi-barrelled pistol.

The man who was dealing the cards, cursed. The other one whistled quietly through his teeth. But the bar's cheap booze had worked its magic and careless bravado emerged.

'That sure looks like one hell of a threat you're holdin' there, Mr Chaf, but nevertheless we still got to protect our employers,' said the man who had told him Broome and Judd were back at the bunk house.

'Yeah, an' we get a bonus for actually doin' it,' the other one joined in, the threat sober and palpable.

The men started sneering, trying to goad and unsettle Hector. But because of the drink, they didn't recognize Hector's gritty resolve, the danger they were both in,

'Hey, Baron, are you goin' to swat this fly,' one of them

said, 'or you lettin' me collect ol' Broome's bounty?'

But now the gunmen had said enough for Hector. It was the inescapable moment he knew would eventually arrive. There was no more time for him; any longer and he'd lose.

'I was only joshin' about this,' he said, his eyes boring deeply into the man directly in front of him. 'It really is a defective ol' piece o' junk. But *this* ain't.' As he spoke, Hector tossed the old pistol onto the table between the two men. It distracted them for the moment he needed, and he drew his holstered Colt. He fired with cold detachment as his .44 bullets struck home.

Neither of the men managed to get their guns clear of their holsters. Even if they'd been stone sober they wouldn't have beaten Hector. He'd had the vital edge.

From his chair, the man named Baron stared out blearily. 'You did the right thing, mister,' he said slowly. 'It was the goddamn cactus juice that did it. Funny how a bullet in your gut sobers you up.'

'Protectin' Wilshaw Broome ain't a funny way to die,' Hector retorted, as the man closed his eyes.

Hector felt an icy chill run through him. He pulled a knife from his pants pocket, then workmanlike, as if he was marking calves, he took a pinch of lobe from the two dead gunmen. 'Keepsakes,' he muttered, shivered involuntarily as he turned to face the few others who remained in the bar.

'You saw what happened here. If you want answers, there's two dead ladies out at the Lunes' house,' he rasped. 'I'll pay fifty dollars for the collectin' an' buryin'. The county pays ten for these two. Either that, or drag 'em to the end o' town for the crows an' coyotes. You'll have no trouble from the law in this godforsaken place.'

Hector stood in the street, took a few deep breaths, as if waiting to take on anyone else who tried to stop him. Then he mounted the claybank, started on a long, curving ride back to the Standing K.

Far to the north, a fork of lightning suddenly split the black sky, then thunder rolled down from the Chuska Mountains. 'It's headed here, 'cause this ain't a good time,' he rumbled miserably. 'What the hell's goin' on?'

As if on cue, it was Judd Kettle who met him halfway between the corral and the main house.

'I reckon Pa's dyin',' he said with remarkable aloofness. 'I've sent someone for the doc, but he's been sayin' it's *you* he wants to see.'

The detachment of Judd's message threw Hector's train of thought, struck him an additional and unwanted blow. And he'd arrived too late, never got to hear what it was that Hoope wanted to see him about. It was only for him to wildly speculate on. Then, a week later, six miles downstream, the half-drowned body of a Mexican wrangler was found under a cut-bank of the Rio Bonito. But no one in Lemmon or out at the Standing K ranch ever got to hear of it.

Treachery pervaded the Standing K. It was a vulture treading the high beams of the ranch house, standing menacingly atop the water vane, circling low above the corrals and home pasture. It was an all-pervading shadow wherever men rode and worked or talked together.

It was some time before Hector got round to asking Wilshaw Broome and Judd Kettle about the deaths of Clemente Lunes and her mother. But they both shook their heads indifferently, never gave an inch towards regret or even concern. Both of them held the opportune thought that Hector believed the murders were the grisly work of their paid gunmen, the reason for him taking revenge in the dog-hole saloon. But Hector had always known who was responsible.

Judd grew more sullen, and it was for some reason other than the death of his father. But he took more control of the ranch workings, frequently by-passed both his foreman and Jasper. His mother arranged for a monthly share income to be paid into a bank in Salt Lake City, Utah, where she now lived with her sister.

These were gloomy days for Hector, but he stuck it out for Jasper as he'd done for Hoope. Besides, he believed there was no other place for him to go; that the Standing K was his home. He saw even less of his old friend Ben, who was paying full attention to a growing family and the care for his land. 'My own little world of league and labour,' he called it. 'What some folk would call "hoot-owl hollow",' was always Hector's faked response.

So, taking everything into account, the day eventually came when Hector was gone. Without fuss, he upped and left along with Jasper and his boy Joseph, who was now nearly ten years old. Ben did get word from his old friend – a letter posted from Westwater Bend, a border town along the Colorado River, but it contained no explanation. As it affected them all, Ben found the years weren't getting any longer. As they rolled by, there remained plenty to occupy his time and thoughts.

10

Ben McGovren's lanky hair was now ash-grey, and his skin was the colour and texture of rawhide. But his eyes retained their bright, piercing darkness. He was jogging along a flat winding trail, his legs clasping the barrel of his favourite clear-foot mare. He crossed the Rio Bonito, rode on to where one remaining grove of live oaks sheltered the spread of his log cabin. As he swung down from the saddle, he looked towards the girl who was rubbing the nose of a fine looking sorrel.

'Ho there, Megan. How's Ma's ague?' he asked in a dusty croak.

'She's OK, Pa. You know she's always a tad improved when you're out of earshot. You get the mail?'

'Yeah, a letter from Westwater. The one I told you about.' Ben pulled the letter from inside his jerkin, handed it to his daughter.

'Ain't that where. . . ?' Megan started to ask.

'Yeah, you go an' read it,' Ben replied quickly.

Dear Ben,

I would have written you sooner, but the river's in spate and there's been no mail transfer for a while. Joe's here, and I showed him your letter. He favours it, says he would have been there long ago, if I had ever told him. It don't sound like

50

much of a hoe dig in the old pear country, so I guess I'll just remain here, kicking heels with the younker. Can't change the habits of a lifetime eh? No, that's me joshin' you, Ben. We'll even trail this letter pretty close, maybe take us a car from Grand Junction all the way to Flora Vista. That's still a ways from Lemmon, but we'll make it soon enough.

Yours truly,
Hector

'Do you know what he's writin' about, Pa? What it means?' Megan asked, handing the letter back to her father.

'Yeah, I know. It means Hector an' young Joe are takin' a railway car. As far as they can, anyway. Take off the post time, an' they could be here real soon.'

'You ain't yet said why, Pa.'

'You get yourself into the saddle, Megan. We'll take us a ride to the Muleshoe tank, an' I'll *tell* you why ol' Hector an' the boy Joe are comin' back.'

Ben waited for Megan to drag on a set of well-worn chaps. As he nodded for them to move off, a grimacing, dishevelled woman appeared at the door of their cabin.

'Where you all goin'? You only just got here,' she shrilled.

'Up to the water-hole, Ma. There's saddle stock needs bringin' in,' Ben called out, but without looking back.

'Better get back in time to split some logs if you want any supper,' she warned.

With Ben leading, the two riders turned their mounts into an old trail that led through dense pear thicket. Megan wore a battered Stetson that covered her coppery brown hair. Time spent in the saddle had tanned her face too, but unlike her father's, it remained smooth.

Ben stopped when they came out of the thicket, and Megan drew alongside. 'You know, Megan,' he started, 'for givin' me *you*, I'll be ever grateful to your ma. But for most

51

else, it's been a road with some dark colour to it.'

A mile further and they reined in beside the water-hole. Ben dismounted, let his mare drop its head. 'I'm tellin' you this not just because you're my daughter, but because you're one o' the very few what knows when an' how to keep a mouth closed when it oughtn't be open,' he said. 'An' that does include your ma, God bless her.'

'But I'm not to tell her whatever it is you're about to tell me, right?' Megan inferred.

Ben nodded and smiled 'Right. It won't improve her disposition, that's for darn sure.'

'What is it can be that serious, Pa?'

'We're broke, Megan. Ruined.'

'What, the ranch? The land? We ain't ever had *money*.'

'The land. I had a talk with the circuit attorney from Gallup. He says the title ain't mine. Never has been. I wanted to find out some time back, but never got round to doin' much about it. He says there ain't any record showin' this land was ever deeded to *my* pa. It still shows as bein' owned by Hoope Kettle's pa,'

'So who does own it *now*?' Megan asked.

'Wilshaw Broome.'

'Wilshaw Broome!' Megan protested, 'How in God's name does he figure in the ownin'?'

'He's got a quit claim deed from Judd Kettle. It was made just before Judd killed himself, and he had it recorded. The lawyer said there's new laws that protect gifted titles, but I never had one in the first place.'

'We got nowhere to go other than here, Pa. We ain't got more'n a pot to piss in.'

'You're goin' to have to watch that fancy language o' yours, Megan, if not your sentiment. Even so, there is a hope.'

'How'd you mean?'

'That pettifogger told me somethin' I don't think he ought to. He said them new title laws come about by bein' in peaceable possession for so many years. Wilshaw Broome's claim comes lawful on Thanksgivin'.'

'Where's the hope in that then, Pa?'

'It's where Hector and Joe come in.'

Megan smiled knowingly. 'I thought the letter would have somethin' to do with it,' she said. 'I recall there weren't any mention o' Joe's pa.'

'Yeah, funny that. But if Hector ain't goin' to mention him, I won't. Not just yet anyways. Do you remember much o' Hector Chaf, Megan?'

Megan nodded. 'Some. He used to duck his head when he came through our door.'

Ben smiled back. 'Yeah, that was him.' Ben pulled up the head of his mount, looked caringly at his daughter. 'I didn't want to have to tell you any o' this, Megan, an' there's still a lot you don't know. Most of it's history, but that don't mean it's gone an' forgot. In fact, there's a whole barnload o' stuff that's happened that I ain't too sure about. Maybe we'll all find out before the end o' November.'

'If we ain't got that much, or never had it, it can't be *that* bad,' Megan suggested.

'Losin' everythin's pretty bad, Megan. Our very way o' life. An' now I'm thinkin' of all the things I coulda done. There's a good school in Albuquerque that I've always known about.'

'I'm turned seventeen, Pa,' Megan said patiently. 'An' what I would've learned there, wouldn't be much good to any of us out *here*.'

'That's my point. A schoolin' could've helped you up in life . . . up an' away from here.'

Megan glanced coyly at her father, 'There's more ways to skin a cat, Pa, if that's what you want,' she said. 'Fact is, I turned down a chance like the one you're talkin' about, just this very day.'

'You did? How come?'

'A rich man's son, by the name o' Felix Broome. He asked me to his wife.'

'He asked you to *marry* him?'

'Yep, bold as brass, just up an' made the proposition.'

'What did you tell him?'

'I said I'd think it over.'

'Well, I don't reckon how I'd manage here without you, Megan, but I'd sure give it a try if you're goin' for happiness. Of course, if you did marry the offspring o' Wilshaw Broome, I'd have to shoot you.'

Megan smiled broadly. 'An' if Felix keeps up the pester, I'll have to shoot *him.*'

Ben returned his daughter's smile, then his expression turned serious. 'Soon after Hector an' Joe get here, there's goin' to be trouble, Megan. We ain't got long.'

'I don't know what you got in mind, Pa, but I'm guessin' whatever it is, it's goin' to happen this side o' Thanksgivin'.'

'Yeah. Just keep what I told you to yourself, Megan. Look out that scattergun o' yours. Better still, don't go ridin' out o' here without tellin' me. Mind you, chances are that I'll be found stretched across some ball o' mesquite before this trouble's over.'

'Na, you won't, Pa. You once said, better a poor livin' than a rich dyin'.'

'Yeah. An' that was before makin' a pile for the Kettles, let alone Wilshaw Broome.' Ben climbed back on the mare. 'That's about all I got to say, Megan, let's go home,' he said, and turned back towards the scrub thickets and the cabin.

11

Although possessing an immense spread with thousands of cattle and horses, Wilshaw Broome didn't build himself a fine new home, or even make a mark on the old one with renovations or improvements. He moved his family into the main house that was once occupied by the Kettle family, but his wife didn't take; she wanted back to the bosom of her family and friends. Now, Broome lived there with his son Felix and a few Mexican servants

The ageing, once-upon-a-time foreman sat in the den with a high beamed ceiling. The November chill was stealing its way across the range, and Broome's features turned ruddy in the reflected firelight from the open hearth. He stirred in his wing-back chair, frowned, grunted at the sound of someone trailing his spurs through the hallway. 'Felix', he muttered. No one else would risk marking the polished oak.

'Pa,' was Felix's simple greeting as he dropped onto a short sofa. 'I thought maybe we could talk. I want to offer some straight goods about my life,' he said, without preamble or the removal of his hat.

Broome looked his son over less companionably than if he'd been a remuda bronc, scanned him from his pale-blue eyes to his neatly shod feet. 'Well, if you do, Lemmon will be all the poorer for it. Specially the tinhorn gamblers you're so fond o' donatin' my money to,' he answered sarcastically.

'I knew you'd scoff, Pa, but this time, it's different. I didn't really decide, it just sort o' happened. The feelin' hit me, an' that was it. I want to settle down, have a wife an' home.'

'There's some would call that the thunderbolt,' Broome said, while favouring Felix with an incredulous stare. 'If your brain was an egg, I'd say it was addled under that goddamn hat you're still wearin'.'

Felix grimaced, removed his hat before he responded. 'I knew it wouldn't be easy gettin' your approval, Pa, but I'd like it anyway,' he said. 'The girl's Megan McGovren.'

'What?' Wilshaw Broome's eyes took on a curious, alarmed glint.

'Megan. I asked her today. Asked her to marry me.'

'What did she say?'

'She said she'd think it over. Comin' from a well-mannered girl, that's got to mean yes.'

'So how bad do you want all this – the girl, the home, the settlin' down? How's your gut feelin'?'

'I never thought of it in them terms, Pa. It's just some-thin' that I feel when I'm with Meg.' By Felix's sensitive assessment, Broome thought he might have his son cornered. 'Well, I ain't givin' my approval or anythin' else,' he said. 'You really thought I would?'

Felix winced at his father's spoiling. 'No, o' course I didn't. I was just runnin' out some courtesy I picked up from somewhere,' he retaliated. 'What's your difficulty with Megan McGovren?'

'It's the difficulty that *you're* goin' to have with her pa, the moment she tells him your intentions towards her. He'll lay for you with everythin' he's got. The only chance you'll have of a life with young Megan is to wait till the worms are feedin' off his scrawny ol' hide.'

56

'We'll just up an' marry. I'm prepared to take a chance if Megan is.'

'There won't be a chance, Felix. He'll shoot you from the saddle. At the very least go an' see him. Use that new found courtesy to pay your respects. See his reaction for yourself.' Broome waited for a second, while his opinion sank in. 'An' I don't blame you for wantin' Megan McGovren,' he added. 'Now get, I still got me some business thoughts.'

When Felix had left the room, Broome turned back to the fire, closed his eyes on his new problems. Goddamn Ben MeGovren, was his immediate thought. Less than a month to go until my title's good, an' he still ain't talkin' to me. He's got somethin' up his sleeve, that's for sure. Although, if his boy was enamoured of the man's daughter, maybe he had an advantage. Hmm, but just *where* and *when*, he schemed.

Early next morning Ben McGovren was saddling his horse, when Megan came out. She drew the mare's head towards her, while Ben fastened the cinch.

'Megan, there ain't much I ever told you not to do,' he said thoughtfully, 'but I got to make sure you don't go ridin' the thickets for a few days.'

'I know, you already told me, Pa,' Megan replied. 'So where are *you* ridin' to?'

'Lemmon. It ain't likely that Hector an' Joseph will turn up there, but I've got to go see. They might need mounts.'

'You told me it would be *you* found dead in the thicket, not *me*.'

'Think, Megan. I was talkin' about events *after* the trouble, not *before*.'

A few minutes later, Megan watched her father ride across the river. I never saw him so tired and worried, she mused. He only hints at stuff, the stuff I don't know about.

For heaven's sake why can't one of us amount to something? If *I* had, I can't see Felix Broome thinking I'd want to marry him. She shook her head sadly, turned away as Ben disappeared into the trail that cut through the pear and mesquite.

Back at the cabin, she turned the other horses out on the range, left her own mount in the corral. She would much rather be riding out than staying close and listening to the trials and tribulations of her mother. But her father had asked her, and she wouldn't flout his request. She had long known of hostility between her father and Wilshaw Broome; in more recent years, had supposed it to be the explicable envy of a cockle-bar cow outfit. Now she knew there was something more behind the hostility, something to do with the land. It was her pa blaming Broome for losing the 'little world of league and labour' that for so many years, he thought he had inherited. She also knew that if her pa was in danger for that 'blame' it would only be on her account.

As the hours dragged on, Megan's concern persisted. She expected Ben to return shortly after midday, so after a bite of lunch, she went back to the corral and with growing unease saddled her horse. But then she climbed up on the corral fence and looked out across the creek to the mesquite through which the clearing ran. She sat there for nearly an hour, until she caught a glimpse of something moving through the brush. She watched until she could see the mount that was swerving erratically towards the creek, and barely a half-mile distant. She swung from the corral, was quickly astride her own horse, and she rode to just beyond the creek, where she almost ran headlong into Ben's mare. The animal was fractious and jumpy from its run, was trailing ribbons of foam across its sweating neck. Megan herded it into a tight circle, and pushed it back along the trail in the direction of Lemmon.

About halfway between the McGovren cabin and Lemmon, the trail crossed a long draw that ran into the Rio Bonito. The broad, flat-bottomed gully was thickly grown over with mesquite, vine and catclaw, and Megan's horse stopped short, snorted its displeasure. The girl dismounted and, catching Ben's still frightened horse, she stood looking about her, groaned audibly when she recognized Ben's Colt .44 by the side of the trail.

She noticed the near empty bottle of Jim Beam and the scuffle marks in the dust as she picked up the Colt. She could see the gun hadn't been fired, and cursed for an explanation. Perhaps the mount ain't such a clear foot as we all thought. 'Yeah, that'll be it,' she muttered wretchedly, knowing that it wasn't, and not understanding the whiskey bottle. She was on the point of tethering the horses and taking a look around when she heard the rumble of hoofs from the direction of Lemmon. Almost immediately, two dust-covered riders appeared through the brush and reined in within thirty feet of Megan. There was no need to ask or wonder who they were, she just knew.

12

The men were well mounted, and each carried a plain-to-see Colt at his belt, and a carbine in a saddle scabbard. From the way he sat the saddle, one of them was very tall and featured a drooping, iron-grey moustache. The other was a young, amenable-looking man with clear blue eyes.

'You in some sort o' trouble, ma'am?' the older man enquired.

The nip of alarm ebbed away as Megan became more certain of the men's identities. 'No,' she said as confident as she could. 'This is my pa's horse, but it's comin' home without him.'

'Hmm, maybe *he's* in trouble then,' the man suggested. 'Is that your pa's Colt that you dropped when you saw us?'

'Yes. But it hasn't been fired. I didn't want you thinkin'. . .' Megan was saying.

The man shook his head as if to say that he wasn't thinking anything. 'You just stay here,' he said. With that, he dismounted and went to take a closer look at the nearby thickets. Megan stood and waited with the young man who had yet to say anything. He studied the area that surrounded them, watching intently, taking in everything.

A few minutes later, the older man returned. 'Which way did you expect your pa to come from?' he asked Megan.

'Lemmon,' she answered, pointing in the direction of town.

The man gave a kindly smile. 'Yeah, I know where Lemmon is,' he said. 'An' how about you?'

'My name's Megan McGovren. Ben McGovren is my father. We got some land an' a homestead not far from here.'

The man smiled again and nodded knowingly. 'Well, my name's Hector Chaf. The big button here is Joseph Kettle, an' I'd be a mite surprised if that didn't mean somethin' to you.'

Megan nodded back. 'It does. Pa got a letter an' he's been expectin' you. Have *you* come from Lemmon?'

The man eyed Megan keenly. 'So you're the McGovren kid, eh?' he considered. 'You was no more'n knee-high, the last time I saw you. I guess time really does work wonders. No, we ain't been *to* or come *from* Lemmon, an' for good reason. We struck this trail about a mile back, an' I wish it had been sooner. Your pa an' me once knew just about every inch o' this country, so maybe it's because o' that, an' the fact that none of us are gettin' any younger, that he's just nodded off in the saddle. His horse got spooked an' down he went. Chances are he's curled up around here somewhere too darned embarrassed to show his face. Now we're here, you let us go find him. If we ain't in your front yard come sundown, meet us back here.'

Megan glanced at Joe, and he nodded his own approval. She remounted and took the bridle of Ben's horse from him. She smiled weakly and without another word, turned back along the trail.

When Megan was well clear, Joe pointed to the bottle. 'Sleepin' it off under the brush, more'n likely, if he's sucked the life from that bottle,' he said jokily.

Hector shook his head. 'No, that's not what happened. I

61

reckon the party's got itself started without us, goddamn it.'

Hector picked up the trail again and they followed it only for a short distance before he spurred for more speed. They forded the Rio Bonito where the prickly pear grew tall and he moved carefully on through the rough country for another half-mile.

'See that big oak risin' over there?' he indicated Joe. 'Well, that's where we're headed, In this rubbish we're workin' close, so leave your carbine.'

The men stopped, quietly loose tethered the mounts they'd purchased at the station yard in Flora Vista. They stole forward through the pear, stopping occasionally to listen, wait for the cicadas and quail to re-settle. They were only a short way off the big oak, when they heard the shouting.

'Coffee's goin' to run out before full dark, food after breakfast.' Ben McGovren's voice carried. 'If you don't feed *me* you'll get yourselves a whole day. What in hell's name are you pair o' turkeys goin' to do after that?' he shouted.

'Huh, I guessed this is where he'd be if he was anywhere,' Hector muttered to himself. 'Didn't guess he'd be in company, though.'

Hector and Joe inched closer. Through a break in the vegetation, a line shack stood hard against the trunk of a live oak. Two horses with dragging bridles were half hidden by a stand of tall cordgrass. They were nosing a ribbon of water that was a run off from the Rio Bonito, Two men stood at the open door, and Ben was sitting just inside, his hands bound, his knees drawn up against his chest. Of the two men, one was an American, the other carried the looks and garb of a Mexican.

'We'll be gettin' another visitor, soon. You'll be more obligin' before the moon comes up,' the American rasped.

'Who the hell's he talkin' about?' Hector said, as he

waved Joe forward. The two men advanced quickly on the shack, their guns thrust forward, menacing the two captors.

'Don't move,' Hector shouted. 'Ben, you old goat, it's *me*. Me an' young Joe Kettle's come to get you. Joe, cut him loose,' he added

Hector turned on the other two men, roughly pushed one up against the other. 'Do I shoot you without knowin' who an' why?' he snapped at them.

'I'm havin' a say at what happens to *them*,' Ben rasped, as he got to his feet. He rubbed at the parts that were aching and sore, then relieved the men of their holstered Colts.

'We ain't done any more'n what we was told to do,' the American growled.

'Hah, so that makes it OK, does it, you sons o' bitches? Who was it gave you your orders then?' Hector demanded.

'An' we don't talk,' the Mexican toughed.

'That's real gritty. Real gritty, an' very, very stupid,' Hector retorted, then turned to his old friend. 'Ben, you got a daughter who's more'n a tad worried about your welfare,' he said. 'No doubt your wife too, by now. You an' Joe go back to the horses. Leave theirs, but take the guns. I'll be with you in a few minutes.'

'What are you goin' to do with *them*?' Ben asked with an edge of anticipation.

'Make sure they're tucked up safe an' sound. We don't want 'em to follow just yet, do we?' Hector shoved the two men inside the shack, indicated for them to stand against the wall opposite the door. 'Ben McGovren's been my friend for a long time, an' he don't deserve to be pig-strung by the likes o' you.' he said threateningly. 'But so far it's all you done, an' I'm takin' that into account.'

The American was suddenly concerned, 'What you goin' to do?' he asked.

'If you take a look, you'll see this is a shack that's got a hole in each of its corners,' Hector explained. 'They been chewed by cotton rats, maybe a coon who's after the cowboys' food store. Who knows, maybe a sidewinder got himself a home here.'

'I don't like any o' them,' the Mexican said uneasily.

'Yeah, for good reason,' Hector said, and stepped outside. He kicked the door to and threw across the retaining bar. 'Maybe your kickin' an' hollerin' will bring a big ol' cougar to eat your mounts.' Then he looked around him, dug deep into his pants pocket to feel a small canvas pouch he'd been keeping there.

'You hurtin' anywhere, Ben?' Hector asked, when he returned to find him and Joe waiting in silence with the horses.

'Maybe some place you can't see,' he said, suppressed anger showing darkly in his eyes. 'Lucky for them fellers you showed up when you did.'

'Yeah, I reckon they're seein' it that way too,' Hector agreed with an ironic grin. 'We found your horse, an' signs o' where you must've had a scuffle.'

'Yeah, I thought you must've done,' Ben gruffed. 'I was on the way back from town when I met up with 'em. Their names are Buscar an' Tate, who's a straw boss to Broome. He pulled a bottle that's got a couple o' fingers left, an' invites me to take a drink with him. "Cut the dust", he says. Before I could refuse, they was real close, one each side o' me. Next thing I knew, the Mex was pressin' a Colt to my kidneys. Weren't much I was goin' to do in them circumstances.'

'So what *did* happen?' Hector asked.

'Tate took *my* Colt an' tossed it to the ground with the bottle. He told me to get off my horse, an' he smacks it for home, says for him an' Buscar to take me on to the line shack.'

'What did they want? What was you supposed to be tellin' 'em?'

'While they're tyin' me up, Tate asks what I know about the title to the Standin' K. Well, I know as much as the ol' iron pot, an' tell him so. But then he offers to turn me loose if I give him the information. Which is kind o' curious, don't you think?'

'I think the son-of-a-bitch got wind o' somethin' an' wanted to trade it on,' Hector suggested. 'An' right now, this ain't the healthiest place for us to sit jawbonin'. I'm hell certain it's Wilshaw Broome that's on the way here, an' we can't take a chance on him bein' alone.'

'I'd take a chance,' Ben rasped.

'Yeah, sure you would,' Hector agreed. 'Meantime, get up behind me, an' let's ride. You follow us real tight, Joe,' he added. 'If you see somethin' move, shoot it. There's likely more bandits an' their snaky kin in this brush than there is thorns.'

Before first dark, they came to where Ben had been kidnapped. Megan was calmly sitting on her horse waiting for them. 'What happened?' she asked impatiently, before anyone else could explain.

As if rehearsed, Ben was ready with his reply. 'Hello, Megan. I was timber drunk,' he excused himself. 'I guess it was the strain got to me. I fell, an' went to the creek to get sobered up. That's where Hec and young Joe found me. That's about it, an' I'm real sorry.'

'That's the story, is it?' Megan asked tetchily.

'Not the full one, no.'

'Let me guess,' Megan retorted. 'These two are honey-dew drummers who got lost between Gallup an' Albuquerque?'

With a touch of fatherly pride, Ben smiled at his daughter. 'Not quite, lass,' he said. 'But if anyone wants to know, they're stock buyers from Denver, Colorado. They'll be stayin' with us for a night or two, an' we're off to look at some breed mares in the mornin'. Now, let's ride. It's gettin' late, an' you never know, your ma might be worried.'

Aboard his mare again, and only a little sore from being tightly trussed, Ben rode on ahead with Hector. Joe didn't appear to notice that Megan was there. She glanced at him from time to time, observed his continued interest in what was going on around, that he did look prepared to shoot if anything moved. She compared him to Felix Broome, intrigued that she should feel so different. She felt in some way superior to Felix, but in no way was that true of Bruno Joseph Kettle.

It was close to full dark when they arrived at the McGovren cabin. 'Of no interest to you, Aileen, they're stock contractors,' Ben said. 'Huh, they ain't even got interestin' monikers.'

After supper the three men went for a stroll around the yard. Megan knew her father would tell her what they were talking about when the proper time came. Her ma wasn't one for exchanging 'snag tales', as she called daily tribulations. For many years she carried a chip on her shoulder at what she'd let herself in for. Once upon a time, Aileen had wanted little more than a comfortable home, and a few fine things to go in it. Ben wanted a homely wife, and a son. So far, neither of them had been truly successful with those wants.

13

'I was tellin' young Joe that someone started the dance before the fiddlers come,' Hector drawled, as the three men stood lee side of the corral chute where they couldn't be overseen or overheard.

'An' I was tellin' you, *I* didn't start nothin',' Ben McGovren countered. 'An' why should I have thought someone was watchin' me?'

'With a section in this godforsaken country, you should be watchin' everythin',' Hector suggested. 'You forgettin' history?'

'Yeah,' Ben agreed. 'I guess I did for a bit.'

'I heard a rumour they got law stretchin' most o' the way across the plateaux now,' Hector continued. 'It just ain't ever broke through the brush to get *here*. I was sort o' hopin' there'd be a filed suit against Wilshaw Broome, an' the law would take its course.'

'Hah, you weren't hopin' any such thing, Hector Chaf,' Ben snorted. 'It's pretty plain now, we pay ourselves fightin' wages an' that's what you were hopin' for.'

'Yeah, maybe. That an' a touch o' homesickness,' Hec affirmed. 'It's been a few long years since I left here. Weren't long after ol' Hoope had his accident. I recall he made Broome more field assistant than foreman. That fall must've broke somethin' in his head. Don't you reckon?'

'I guess so, Hec, but it's history. An' it don't rightly explain why you rode north with Jasper an' his boy. You sayin' you got upset at what was goin' on between ol' Hoope an' Broome? I reckon right now might be the time to spill.'

'I'll come to that, Ben. An' no, it weren't just because o' the relationship between them two. You know that Judd went sort o' loco, pushed young Jasper from his furrow. But the kid was entitled to a full share and he told Judd as much.'

'Ain't been the first time those brothers fought, Hec, an' you know it.'

'Not to the point where one of 'em orders the other one off the property like some sort o' pariah dog. Jasper got real mad at that, even went for his gun. He wouldn't have shot, but I stopped him anyway, got him to ride into town with me to cool off.'

'An' you didn't stop till you got to Westwater, is that it?' Ben asked quizzically.

'No, you old fool, not quite,' Hector corrected him jovially. 'Out on the road, we met up with Broome an' a couple of his 'punchers. Some words passed between them an' Jasper, who knew Broome to be the guilty one, *an'* Jasper was still pipin' with frustration at havin' almost shot his own kin. One o' the 'punchers lost his nerve an' levelled a big hogleg, but Broome was ahead of him. He read the situation, cursed Jasper some, then ordered his men to ride on – him with 'em. For all his faults, there's a feller who knows when to back off. Young Jasper's face would've told him that, without *me* bein' there.'

'Yeah, I'd have liked to have seen that,' Ben said. 'Go on.'

'Me an' Jasper rode on to Lemmon. We both knew that Broome was a thief. Cattle, land, money, you name it. He always had been, an' we didn't need *that* day's happenin' to drive it home. Jasper couldn't handle bein' in a position where he nearly kills his own brother. He reckoned he ought to get himself out of any situation where it would happen again, as it likely would. He didn't see any gain in hangin' around with his family ties bein' so combustible.'

'So that's when *you* took off?'

'Yeah, the three of us. Joe was ten.'

'You went straight up to Westwater?'

'No, Tacoma. Me an' Jasper got work easy enough, an' Joe went to school.'

'What happened to Jasper?'

'He died. Goddamn yellow fever came in off the summer levels. At least he saw Joe finish his schoolin'. That's when we decided to move on, ended up at Westwater Bend, where I wrote you. When you told me about the land belongin' to Jasper, I had to tell Joe. That changed a lot o' things – for both of us.'

'There's been a hell of a lot o' dyin' west o' the Rockies, Hec. Sounds like you kept movin' just to avoid it,' Ben suggested wryly.

Hector raised his eyes. 'But only for so long. There comes a time. . . .' He trailed off the innate warning.

Ben nodded his understanding. 'You know there's stuff that *I* got to tell,' he offered.

'If it's about Wilshaw Broome, you best tell it,' Hector advised his old friend.

'Broome brought in his wife an' kid from somewhere outside o' Gallup. He got 'em both payrolled with Judd at the ranch house. Some goddamn twist of fate for Judd to go picking daisies not long after; specially after he'd made over a quit claim deed to Broome a day or so before they found him. It looked real fish, Hec, but who was to look into it? Jasper was gone an' there weren't anyone else.'

'How did Judd die?' Hector asked.

'In a manner o' speakin' he drank himself to death. He

went on a bender, fell from his horse, an' broke his neck. There were enough witnesses to say that's how it happened, but there was also one or two that said he was no more roostered than normal.'

'Well, you're right about a heap o' people dyin',' Hector agreed. 'Perhaps we *should* keep on the move. The Rio Bonito's always been a dangerous place to linger.'

'But it's got real valuable in the passin' years,' Ben said. 'It was because I wanted to sell some o' what I got, or *thought* I'd got, that I found out.'

'You mean, found out you got no claim?' Hector wanted to know.

'Yeah, that's right. There's no title of any description. The ol' buzzard didn't even leave a promissory.' Ben shrugged wearily. 'I can only guess it was because that section weren't worth a plugged nickle in them days. Most folk would never have foreseen the value in years to come. Huh, *these* goddamn years.'

'Well, that's why we're here,' Hector rasped drily. 'A few civic adjustments need to be made. You say that new law makes Thanksgivin' the done-by date?'

Ben nodded. 'Yeah. That's when his ten years o' peaceable possession are up.'

'That's about the long an' the short of it, Joe,' Hector said, turning to Joseph Kettle who had remained quiet but very attentive. 'Ain't much doubt Wilshaw Broome got an opportune benefit by the death o' your uncle Judd. An' he's recruited an army o' gunmen to help him keep his ill-gotten gains. He must've known one day you'd be back. Rights an' wrongs never did mean much in this neck o' the woods. As for us, we got three fair mounts, an irregular mix of ordnance, an' a heap o' good intentions. For two of us it'll be just like of times, but what do *you* say?'

Joe looked at Hector. 'Do you remember that school

ma'am in Tacoma? The one who asked me what my child-hood was like, an' I shrugged and said, "*oh, just normal I guess*".' Joe shook his head, grinned at the memory. 'Well, I done enough listenin' to you an' Ben givin' a standpoint to Kettle history, but it is *my* family not *yours*. So if you want that we stick it to 'em, we'll start the chamber spinnin' with a challenge on that title deed. I'll ride into Lemmon tomorrow to file it, maybe buy us some more bullets.'

14

Next morning, Megan was wearing a dress and her hair was brushed loose. She was well worth a second look, and she got it from Joseph when the men sat down for breakfast.

An hour later, when Hector and Joe were saddling up, Ben had a quiet word with her.

'I like it,' he said, and smiled warmly. 'But I said I'd tell you about this mess we got.'

'You can start by admittin' you weren't drunk out there in the brush,' Megan replied.

'Yeah, well, I wasn't,' he said, and told her what had really happened.

'Where are those men now?'

'Hector took care of 'em. Exactly *how*, might be one thing best left alone,' Ben advised.

'What about the land bein' wrested from the Kettle family?'

'We got a pretty good idea it was Wilshaw Broome who murdered Judd Kettle . . . somehow inveigled the Standin' K from him. We're goin' into Lemmon, an' ol' Hoope Kettle's grandson's goin' to file a dispute for the town clerk.'

'But after what happened yesterday, there's still goin' to be a fight. Joe knows that?' Megan speculated.

'As sure as God made little apples. But Hec told me this

boy's the spit of his pa. I know he don't talk much, but I ain't seen a youngster in a while I took to more.'

'I know, an' he ain't said more'n two words to *me* since we met up,' Megan chipped back.

'Well, if he could, Megan, he'd probably say he's pleased you got yourself prettied up for him.'

'I can dress for—' Megan started to protest, but Ben held up his hand.

'It's worth it for whatever, or whoever,' he said. 'Now, if the moment we're gone, you switch that costume to chaps an' boots, remember, I don't want you ridin' out too far. The Broome men won't give a woman any trouble, but if they ain't lookin' too close, they might snap off a long range shot at anyone approaching. I got to go now, Megan. You just remember what I said.'

'I will. But *you* remember that as far as I'm concerned they can have anything except my pa.'

Megan watched the three men ride away and the straight back and broad shoulders of young Joe Kettle. So this was the way her feelings were developing, she considered with interest. She hoped *he* knew it; recalled that soldiers who rode into combat often took a loved one's keepsake with them.

'Why don't you go ridin' with them stock buyers, Megan? You know just as much as your pa about four-legged critters?' Her mother's strident voice brought Megan out of her agreeable reverie. 'You might stop him from bein' robbed blind.'

'I could certainly stop him from somethin',' Megan muttered.

Ten minutes later Megan was into her range clothes, and she was headed for the Rio Bonito. A little smile crossed her ma's face as she watched, waved from the small pantry window. Megan waved back. It wasn't much of a deceit not to say she wasn't riding after her pa and Joe and Hector.

Megan rode along the banks of Rio Bonito. She looked into the breeze-rippled water, watched the slim willow leaves that skimmed across the sheltered eddies. She rode for nearly an hour before reining in where a thick screen of mixed timber ran close to the river-bank. She climbed from her saddle and sat with her back against a gnarled buckeye. For a long time, she stared pensively into the bright running water, felt the press of impending trouble.

A hundred yards upstream, on the opposite bank, a man was talking to his horse, getting it to pull back from the water's edge, 'Stand up,' you ol' soak,' he encouraged.

'What the hell are we doin' up here, Krate?' a second man asked.

'I told you, we're lookin' out for somebody,' Carter Krate answered back. 'It's what the boss wants us to do, so we best do it. You saw the mood he was in earlier.'

'Did he tell you who we're supposed to be lookin' out for?'

'Yeah, an' he said we shouldn't make a ruckus, so keep your goddamn voice down. We're to see if Ben McGovren's got any riders with him.'

'Huh. That old coot ain't likely to be with anyone, less it's his mare. He don't need no help to run that shirt-tail outfit.'

'Well, Felix is sayin' otherwise,' Krate answered back. 'He says McGovren's suddenly got himself a couple o' gun-packers. Do you know where Tate an' Perez were last night?'

'Gettin' roostered in town.'

'No, they weren't,' Krate corrected. 'Felix said his pa found 'em in a line shack by one o' the creeks. He said whatever happened durin' the night got 'em frightened speechless. No good to man nor beast for a day or so. It made Broome madder'n a stuck pig.'

'They must've said somethin'.'

'Yeah, that it was McGovren, but he had two others coverin' his back. That's what we're doin' out here ... lookin' for 'em. Oh, an' somethin else,' Krate added. 'There was what looked like a couple o' corn nubbins stuck to the shack's door on a pear thorn. But they was dried-up earlobes, human earlobes. Boss said it was some sort o' hex, a sign of retribution. Felix reckons that's what's got him rattled, not the treatment two of his riders got.'

'So what are we supposed to do if we run into 'em?'

'That's up to us, I guess. Felix reckons his pa's puttin' up a fat reward for bringin' 'em down.'

'There's all sorts o' *fat*, Krate.'

'Felix reckons it'll be three or four hundred dollars apiece for McGovren an' them two other fellers.'

The other man whistled through his teeth. 'All things bein' equal, that's a fair bounty. An' up against another 'puncher, I'd take it. But how'd we spend more'n a year's pay in Boot Hill, if they're hired guns?'

'Yeah,' Krate agreed. 'We'll have to be real watchful, that's for sure.'

'Any other likely trouble we should bear in mind?'

'No, other than to look out for the girl. She ain't to be harmed.'

'The McGovren girl? What's she got to do with all this?'

'I reckon Felix has gone sweet on her,' Krate said. 'But we'll find out tonight, when we ride to that little house o' theirs. But don't worry yourself into a spin, there's goin' to be a good half-dozen of us.'

'So, what the hell's goin' on?'

'I don't get to know the detail, but accordin' to Felix, if they want to fight fire with fire, we'll oblige.'

'I was meanin' the breadth of it. What's behind it all?'

'Accordin' to Felix, this Ben McGovren's been rustlin'

hereabouts for most of his life. The old Broome's got tired of it, an' wants an end to it, once an' for all.'

'Well, if he has been rustlin', he ain't got too much out of it. I wouldn't have thought McGovren folk were much of a threat.'

'Perhaps not, but I ain't goin' to argue the case,' Krate decided. 'I'm thinkin' more o' them dollars. Let's ride further up the creek.'

15

Lemmon was barely awake when Joe and his two friends rode in. Joe had been thoughtful on the ride down. It was a pushy, challenging thing he was about to do, and at one point he wondered whether to feign a lack of involvement and return to Colorado. But he was soon through it. He and his father before him had been robbed, and he smarted with youthful anger at the thought of it.

He didn't have the help in numbers to play against the thieves, but so what? No one ever had two more loyal and resolute supporters than the two oldsters who now rode with him. Hector Chaf bore a long-time grudge against Wilshaw Broome. Ben was similar in his own list of grievances, coupled with the occupancy of a valuable tract of land. Both men held a powerful loyalty to the Kettle family.

At first glance, the old cow town looked more or less as it had when he was a boy. The early morning sun slanted across the old adobe and false-front buildings, the occasional brick and two-storey structures. But there were a few more, like the grandly named Town Hall, and the double-fronted Agave Hotel. Joe smiled wistfully, recalled playing diabolo in the shade of the mercantile store's awning. He had sat on the steps, thought the travelling salesmen impressive in their dark, store-bought suits.

Joe wasn't normally given to emotional arrests, but now

77

he sniffed, took an affecting swallow. Like it or not, Lemmon was his home town, and he'd come back. He coughed noisily and moved on up the main street.

Chris Tolman was standing at the door of his sun-bleached cantina. It was too early for much passing trade, but Tolman was his own reliable customer for most of the day. Blinking his eyes against the rising sun, he wondered who it was stepping up the Town Hall steps with Ben McGovren.

'Mornin', I'd like to see the clerk,' Joe addressed the man who was sitting at a broad, leather-topped desk. 'The person who takes up issues on land disputes.'

'That'll be me, Brent Perser. I handle most stuff around here of a civic an' legal nature,' the sharp-featured man said.

'I'm talkin' *illegal*, an' I want to file a suit,' Joe continued.

'Well, that's still me. You want to see Lawyer Daggert?'

'I reckon I can handle my part,' Joe replied. 'But someone else might have need of him,' he added with a cold smile.

'Fill in these blanks,' Perser said, and handed Joe some paper from a desk tray.

'Can I use your typewriter?' Joe asked him.

'Typewriter?' Perser echoed, as if he himself didn't understand the word.

'Yeah, we ain't all beaver men you know,' Joe said, his smile easing a fraction. He turned and winked at Hector and Ben who were sharing bemused glances between Joe and the big Remington typewriter. 'The school in Tacoma had an early business semester,' he explained. 'I guess that's somethin' else I owe my pa for.'

Twenty minutes later, Joe returned the paper to Perser. 'Look it over,' he said. 'See if it's clear an' regular.'

'Oh, I'm just sure it is,' Perser answered with a impressed

78

nod. As he read, he made several gruff rumblings in his throat as he stared at the space for signatures. At the bottom of the page, Joe had typed: Witnessed, signed and dated by Hector Chaf and Ben McGovren.

'Er, well yes, that's the right words. But you don't need witnesses for the filing,' Perser informed Joe.

'Perhaps not. But as long as they don't invalidate it, I want 'em there,' Joe told him.

Neither Ben nor Hector had spoken since they had entered the office. They signed their names in continued silence and followed Joe out after he had paid the fees.

'Touchpaper's lit,' Ben growled once they were outside.

'We just put restraint on Wilshaw Broome's title to the Standin' K, nothin' more,' Hector said. 'But it's a filed dispute on the possession an' he can't hide it.'

'You went to that Tacoma school as well, eh Hector?' Ben asked with wry humour.

'Nope. It's just a tad more civilized up in Colorado. Business is an everyday occurrence, even for cowpokes.'

'Wilshaw Broome might now have a disputed possession, but in this godforsaken country, he'll dispute the dispute, an' it won't be by wavin' a piece o' goddamn paper. Just take a look there.' Hector nodded back towards the building where the clerk was locking a side door that he'd pulled to.

'Where the hell's he off to?' Joe asked.

'As a county official who probably stands in line to get paid, I'd say Broome's lawyer,' Ben said.

'Hell, let's get some tonsil juice, while we're here,' Hector suggested. 'I know the ideal place.'

Leading their horses they crossed to the dog-hole saloon that Hector had once notably paid a visit to. 'Remind me to tell you a story about this place, Joe,' he said, as they hitched their mounts.

'Hah, that was folklore for a couple o' years,' Ben

chuckled, as they stepped onto the low boardwalk.

The moment they were through the door, Hector looked quickly around him. He moved to the end of the bar, in the darker light away from the window.

'What's your poison, fellers?' Tolman asked.

'Whiskey,' Hector answered.

Tolman took a closer look at Hector. 'Were you Hector Chaf, before them grey whiskers?' he queried.

Hector levelled back a hard stare. 'Yeah, an' before you got lard gutted, you were the goddamn bigot who never knew the whereabouts o' Quedo Lunes,' he snapped back.

Tolman thought for a moment before responding. 'Sure, I fill up the space a bit more'n I used to,' he said. 'Can't get from the bar to the can as quick, but yeah, that sounds like me.'

'Three glasses,' Hector said, as he cast an eye around the bleak, sparsely furnished saloon.

Tolman placed the glasses on the bar and uncorked a bottle of whiskey. 'Just like ol' times to see you two drinkin' together,' he offered. Then he looked at Joe. 'I used to wear out the knees o' my pants crawlin' an' duckin' away from the bullets.' He shrugged when there was no response from Joe. 'Well, we don't get gun stuff anymore,' he continued, looking from Ben's holstered Colt to Hector's, than Joe's. 'No, sir, them days are long gone.'

'That's why you got singled out,' Hector said. 'Somewhere to relax safely an' in private for a friendly drink.'

Ten minutes later, a group of riders pulled up in the narrow street. They were directly across from the bar, and Ben asked Tolman if he was expecting company.

'Well, I'm always hopin',' the man replied. 'But if it's who I think it is, maybe we're headin' for another memorable moment.'

The old cantina with its thick adobe walls and one dust-caked window at the front was gloomy on the brightest of days, and entering from the street's bright sunlight, the newcomers didn't recognize anyone at first. Wilshaw Broome had gulped down half his first beer before he took an interested look at Hector who was standing less than six feet from him.

'Hector Chaf,' Broome grunted with a touch of alarm. 'Looks like trouble ain't come single-handed.'

Hector took a single step back. 'That's right, Broome. 'Your worst nightmare's suddenly come true,' he returned with hushed menace.

Broome smiled compliantly. 'I ain't come here lookin' for trouble, Chaf,' he claimed and looked to the three men who were with him. 'I mean it. Cover me while I leave,' he told them and immediately edged towards the door.

Ben, who had been standing behind his two companions, then stepped into view.

'Jeesus, it's him. That's McGovren,' Broome said roughly, as he backed through the open door and into the street.

Hector watched him go, cursed because he couldn't shoot him in the back. 'There goes a man who gives a whole new meanin' to "he who shouts an' runs away",' he rasped, and turned back to face the man's three cohorts.

The word was out for Broome's hired men to kill Ben McGovren on sight, but Broome's henchman didn't realize that Ben, Joe and Hector were in cahoots, were the *trouble* that Wilshaw Broome had just been referring to. Influenced by the big dollar reward that Broome was offering, he mistakenly made a move for his gun.

Before he cleared his holster, Joe hit him. He'd drawn his own Colt and laid the frame hard into the side of the man's head. It split the skin from temple to jawbone, and the man went down cold.

81

Ben knew that close-quarter blows were safer than bullets, and he quickly stepped forward to crack the barrel of *his* Colt against the second man's forehead. The man's eyes rolled, went blank before he too crumpled to the rough puncheon floorboards.

Hector caught sight of Tolman moving behind the bar. 'Stay put,' he yelled, while watching Broome's third guard run for the safety of the street.

'It might be best to clear this place,' Ben rasped at Joe and Hector. 'We don't know how many they're goin' to bring down on us now.'

Outside, they just saw the Broome man run into another saloon further along the street. It was a place that Hector had visited all those years before.

Gaining their horses, they were cutting diagonally across the street when the first gun blasted. Then other guns were cracking out and bullets whined and thumped all around them. Hector checked his horse and emptied his Colt at the front of the second saloon. The door splintered apart and he cursed those inside. 'You're gutless scum, Broome, an' I should o' killed you years ago!' he yelled. Then, with Joe and Ben, alongside him, he whirled his horse and raced to the edge of town.

16

A mile beyond the outskirts of town, Joe pulled up his horse. Hector and Ben, thinking maybe he'd been wounded, reined in beside him.

'You ain't hit, are you, son?' Ben asked anxiously.

'No, I'm not hit. I just ain't runnin' any further. We're not goin' to win anythin' this way.'

'An' we ain't winnin' it by gettin' dead, either,' Hector replied sharply. 'Broome's got himself a score o' trigger-itchy thugs back there, an' we only met the advance party. There's no sense in goin' up against a whole gang of 'em, until we know there's a chance, an' that ain't in town or anywhere near it,'

'So where are you thinkin' of?' Joe asked eagerly.

'In the goddamn pear – where else?'

Ben nodded in accord and heeled his mare forward. They rode on and, although frustrated, Joe followed doggedly in the rear. Markers had been put down and both sides knew where they stood, but if any Broome riders wanted to follow, he'd have first sighting. Given his head, he'd go back and dust the town's foundations if it had any.

Back in Lemmon, Joe had been right about someone else needing the services of the lawyer, George Daggert. After leaving the saloon, Wilshaw Broome had stood in the street for a moment, shaking with fury when he saw the man he wanted rid of, clear the end of town with his armed allies. A minute or two later, he'd made it to the town's law office.

'Are you comin' *from*, or headin' *to* trouble?' Daggert asked, as Broome came through the door, choking on blasphemies.

'*Both*,' Broome stormed. 'Them boys o' mine had Ben McGovren cold, then let him get away.'

'Well, it couldn't have been so cold, Wil. But don't go blowin' a plug, the man's got away before. It's a habit o' his an' he don't usually get far. Was it Hector Chaf an' Jasper Kettle's boy who got away with him?'

'Yeah, how'd you know that? How'd you know it was one o' the Kettles?'

'Comes with my territory,' the lawyer said. He waved the paper he held in his hand and explained the filing of the suit.

'Burn it. Goddamn piece o' paper,' Broome snapped.

'He'd best not,' Brent Perser said, who was keeping prudently close. 'If this case ain't on the docket when the court next meets, an' them three fellers swears it was filed, it won't just be *me* takin' a trip to Yuma.'

'Them turkeys won't be swearin' to anythin', 'Broome continued angrily. 'Not if I get another chance at 'em.'

'Brent's right,' Daggert said forcefully. 'There's more'n just *your* livelihood at stake here, Wil, an' you can't blame anybody but yourself. But that's only for us to know, so calm down an' listen to sense. I told you two months ago that McGovren had somethin' up his sleeve.'

'Yeah, an' I tried to get him to talk about it.'

'An' he didn't, but no one's burnin' anythin' because o' your hot-headedness,' Perser charged, and put the paper in his pocket. 'Goin' up against county law's one thing I hadn't bargained on.'

'Are you thinkin' o' givin' up bein' clerk to this town?' Broome threatened.

Perser flinched. 'You an' this town need me more'n I need either o' *you*, an' that's a *fact*,' he retorted. 'To date, how many o' your boys have them three "turkeys" done for?'

'They ain't done for any of 'em,' Broome said, suddenly less aggressive.

'That's the point,' Daggert said with a trace of exasperation. 'Don't it tell you somethin' about 'em? I'm tellin' you now, Wil, if you want the job done your way, go ahead an' do it your way. But if that youngster's only got half the sand of his pa, an' he has teamed up with Chaf and McGovren, you've got real trouble.'

'An' you best be real sure o' your men,' Perser put in. 'Bein' dead's bad enough, but there's some would say that gettin' beat up an' humiliated's worse.'

Daggert nodded, continued the argument. 'Them fellers ain't within jurisdiction as long as they're in the pear thicket,' he advised. 'An' now they know what you got in mind, it stands to reason, that's where they'll be lyin' for you.'

Broome gritted his teeth and his features paled. Maybe Daggert and Perser were right. But then again he could double bluff. Sure, McGovren and his friends had run for home, but he would step up the reward for bringin' them in. And there wouldn't be any of that dead or alive nonsense either. His men would act fast, probably get them before full dark. With his tormentors out of the way, he felt a brief degree of safety. The man made his way from the lawyer's office to issue instructions about taking care of his two wounded men, to increase payments on his own safety.

'You better lock that paper up good. I recommend somewhere you can't even find it yourself,' George Daggert wryly suggested to Perser, the moment Broome had left his office.

'County Sessions meets first Monday o' the New Year, an' if any one o' that Kettle gang's still kickin', you'll need it.'

'Broome'll take care of 'em. He's got too much to lose if he don't.'

'The same can be said o' Ben McGovren an' the Kettle kid,' Daggert pointed out. 'Thanksgivin's just about on us, an' to flush McGovren an' Chaf out o' that brush country ain't goin' to be no hunt the thimble. Wilshaw Broome's messed up on his best chance, an' you know why?'

'Yeah, 'cause underneath that bark, there's a goddamn milk-liver.'

'We won a couple o' skirmishes, but that don't mean much,' Hector Chaf said, when they were another mile or so out of town. 'Not all Broome's hired thugs will be in the mould o' those we already tangled with. But I already promised myself one thing, fellers: if ever I get that close to him again, I'll add a few more holes to those he started out with. The Good Lord won't think any the worse o' me, I'm sure.'

'No more'n he probably does already,' Ben jibed.

'I just might have somethin' to do with that pledge o' yours,' Joe said. 'I'd rather he relinquished his claim . . . hear him say the words. It would sound good, an' sure save a lot o' trouble . . . maybe a few lives.'

'*He'll* save himself a lot a trouble if he ever sees you when you ain't lookin, *that's* for sure,' Ben snorted.

'That's right,' Hector agreed, peering across the surrounding scrub. 'This pear country's full of his hirelin's, an' if we don't sharpen up, they'll flush us like quail.'

'We're sharp enough, Hec,' Ben said. 'What's your meanin'?'

'There's a rider goin' to cross our trail in a moment or two,' Hector answered quietly. He eased his carbine in its scabbard, nodded his head to the left of where they were grouped, 'Who do we know who can pick their way safely through this fearsome stuff?' he added.

'Aileen an' Megan,' Ben said without hesitation. 'An' that's Aileen. I'd know that cloud watcher o' hers, anywhere.'

And so it was Ben's wife who rode up to them. Beneath her broad-brimmed, straw-weave hat, her eyes showed surprise then defiance.

Ben was obviously taken aback. 'Where you goin', Aileen?' he asked uncertainly.

'Lemmon. I left you a note,' she rattled back. 'I'm tired o' this godforsaken place with nothin' but sawflies an' hog-noses for company. I'd like to talk to someone, eat a served-up meal that don't include beef or biscuit.'

'Is this you sayin' you're leavin' me, Aileen?' Ben asked in an uncharacteristic, discomfited manner.

'That depends. I'll go right back to Las Cruces if you really can't provide better than you done so far, Ben McGovren. Only this time it ain't the same ol' threat.'

'Aw, come on, Ma,' Ben appealed. 'Right now, I got some important business to take care of. I'll come an' get you when we're sorted, an' we'll talk it through.'

Aileen pondered her husband's suggestion for a moment. Then she shook her head sadly and pulled her horse back to the town trail.

Joe looked from Hector to Ben in stricken amazement. Hector gave a considerate smile, but none of them spoke because there was nothing they could think of to say.

17

'I guess there's no pleasin' some people,' Ben said resignedly. 'Do you remember Quedo Lunes, Hec?'

'Yeah, of course. He was a decent feller who usually had somethin' perceptive to say,' Hector replied.

'Yeah. He once said, "Pick the wrong woman, Ben, an' she'll throw more out with her spoon than you can bring in with your shovel".'

'Prophetic as well,' Hector returned. 'Did anyone ever find out what happened to him?'

'No, not really. But a few years ago, I heard rumour of a crazy old man with long white hair, stalkin' the pens outside o' Fort Wingate. He was gabblin' an' beggin' for quarters. I got to thinkin' that, if Quedo had returned home that night to find his wife and daughter the way *I* did, *that* would o' twisted his mind some.' Ben shuddered, and heeled his mare onward once again.

Hector took an examining glance at his old side partner. Witnessing Aileen's state of mind, her behaviour, he wondered if the wild pear thickets and the brooding on his failures hadn't touched Ben likewise. How on earth could he take the fact so coolly that his wife was threatening to leave him? Could it really have been Aileen's righteous anger that had brought Quedo Lunes into his mind?

Carefully watching the thickets on both sides of the trail, the three riders continued towards the McGovren homestead. As they approached the clearing where Ben had been jumped the day before, Ben held up his hand. 'An' here comes the other one who knows the country,' he rasped. 'I wonder if she's throwin' in her lot.'

Megan's horse was covered with sweat and its sides were heaving.

'That colt's too young to be rode that way, Megan,' Ben said, noting that his daughter's hand was slipped around the stock of her scattergun. 'You know somethin' we don't?'

Megan shook her head. 'Just a feelin'. I had to come lookin' for you. Have you seen Ma?'

'Yeah, we met up aways back, I got . . . we *all* got the impression she was discontented, an' I can't say I blame her,' Ben replied. 'An' she don't even know that Wilshaw Browne is evidently offerin' a reward for our scuts.'

'As if we're a family o' cottontails,' Hector added sourly.

'I've had a thought that ain't too unrelated,' Joe said, eyeing Megan considerately as he spoke. 'It ain't right that you're losin' your home, just to win back mine. If I go an' unfile that suit, take ol' Hec here back to Westwater, maybe it'll put a stop to all this.'

'Sorry, Joe, too late for maybe,' Ben differed. 'Sure, it ain't right that our home's bein' done away with, but yesterday when they laid into me, they had no idea you were involved. Coyotes could be chewin' on my bones right now if you hadn't arrived.'

'Yeah,' Hector agreed, 'this really ain't your doin', Joe, an' all of us are involved. Anyway, you wouldn't get to withdraw that suit. They're watchin' the town, an' have you in their sights the moment you break cover. Let's get on to Ben's house, prepare for our own little Alamo.'

They rode for another five miles, but Joe said he wasn't hiding behind anybody, and now he rode ahead with Hector.

'Do you reckon your ma means it?' Ben asked his daughter. 'Do you reckon she is on the way to Las Cruces? Am I that bad, Megan?'

'Well, Ma reckons so, Pa. But she would be in the way here, an' there's danger. For the time bein', look at it that she's best off in town.'

'That's how I'm lookin' at it for you, Megan. I'm thinkin' o' sendin' you after her.'

'You think on, Pa. I'm here for the full party.'

Ben accepted Megan's decision, so he asked about Felix Broome's proposal. 'You made up your mind yet about young Felix?'

'Yes, I have,' Megan said. 'There's somethin' about him, one or two things he's intimated. Maybe it's by mistake, but I got to wonderin' just how much difference there is between him an' his pa. So for the time bein' I'm throwin' in with you, Pa.'

With that, Megan rode on in silence, divided her time between encouraging her weary colt, and making another thoughtful study of Joe Kettle's back.

Ahead, Hector was talking with Joe. 'I told you this place was wild, Joe,' he said.

'Yeah, I ain't seen much like this before,' Joe replied. 'An' Ben's mighty het up about somethin'. I'd say more'n what he's been tellin' us. He'd have taken 'em all on, if we hadn't arrived. What do you think, you know him?'

'Thought I did, Joe. Still, it won't be many more hours before we find out. I must admit, I ain't too happy about havin' the girl around.'

'I'm not too happy about bein' here myself, Hec. But, from what I seen an' heard, I reckon she can handle herself well enough.'

Ben caught up with Megan, waited until she looked at him before he spoke. 'Looks like it's down to you an' me,

Megan,' he said with a friendly smile.

'You an' me, what?' Megan asked.

'*Me* to quarter a pair o' hung calves, *you* to make supper. O' course you could change your mind an' ride back to Lemmon.'

Two hours later, Megan loaded an enormous platter of biscuits and fried beef onto the scrubbed pine table.

'Looks like Mrs McGovren might have had a point,' Joe asided to Hector as they sat down.

'You weren't thinkin' o' feedin' the Broome boys when they get here, were you, Megan?' Hector jibed.

'No. I'm just expectin' us all to be here for breakfast,' she answered back with a smile.

'I been thinkin', an' I might have somethin' to say on that score,' Ben advised them.

Hector and Joe exchanged puzzled glances, then began the serious task of forking their meal.

Hector looked around him as they ate. Kitchen scullery and living quarters was an all-in room, and there were two others adjoining at the back. Outside, between two small stock corrals, there was a food store, a low open-sided barn and a shed.

'How sure are we that they're bringin' the fight out here?' Joe asked, after a sip of his strong, hot coffee.

'Well, where else?' Ben responded. 'We sort o' narrowed down their opportunities.'

'How do you reckon they'll get to us, Ben?' Joe asked.

'The way we're primed in here, they'll have to burn us out, Apache fashion.'

'An' why tonight?'

'Because the iron's hot. It's one o' the things that Wilshaw Broome knows about,' Hector contributed. 'Ben's right, an' they won't give us time organizin' a defence, either.'

At the best of times, the McGovrens hadn't much in the way of leisure pursuits or conversation, and most nights were spent in tired sleep. But now, Ben's thoughts about their resistance took a different turn. 'I got me an idea,' he said. 'It could be a way to come out o' this battle, alive an' kickin'. At full dark we douse lamps an' keep real quiet.'

'Yeah, so just tell us the way it's goin' to be, Ben,' Hec said, and smiled encouragingly.

'This old shack ain't worth makin' a fight for, even it was mine. But it ain't, an' won't ever be, the way things stand now,' Ben started. 'You think I don't know that Ma was right? Huh, the goddamn place is fallin' apart.'

Megan poured more coffee, while Ben shaped his thoughts and his strategy. 'If we stand 'em off tonight, they'll come back, an' keep comin' back,' he told them. 'So, if Broome does reckon to fire the cabin, we'll turn the tables on him. We'll stay ahead.'

'If you mean what I think you mean, the answer's no,' Joe protested. 'You're not makin' sacrifices like that in my fight,'

'I already told you, son, as far as me an' mine are concerned, it's *my* fight,' Ben chided. 'An' it was before yours.' With that, Ben explained his plan, summarily started its preparation.

The second of the two hung calves was cut into quarters, and the hide was cut into five parts. Into the five pieces of rawhide, the head, together with the big cuts of meat, were wrapped. A few smaller bones and some fabric scraps from Aileen McGovren's makeover chest were added for good measure.

'Them firebugs won't be stayin',' Ben muttered. 'Half a look at these beauties, an' they'll be runnin' scared for the rest o' their lives.'

The gruesome bundles were dragged into the house, and

three of them were heaped where Ben, Joe and Hector would likely be defending from. The other two were placed at the back of the cabin where the women would most likely be taking shelter.

Each of the five would-be defenders took a blanket and left-over beef and biscuit and set off to find concealed vantage points. For a moment Ben looked back into the darkness of the cabin. He thumbed the matches deep in his pants pocket, nodded at what he considered to be an effective preparation. 'You didn't think we'd eat our way through two o' my weaners, did you?' he smiled grimly at Hector.

A long and nervy hour later, four men emerged silently from the thicket trail. They moved cautiously towards the house, stopped to listen, then crept closer. Watchful for any sight or sound, their full attention was fixed ahead. They had almost reached the open door, when one of them felt the barrel of Megan McGovren's scattergun stabbing them low and painful in the back. The three others turned to be confronted by the guns of Joe Kettle, Hector and Ben.

'If one o' you was Wilshaw Broome, I'd shoot everyone, here an' now,' Ben rasped at them. 'So take advantage o' the situation, an' drop your weapons . . . all o' you.'

The four men surrendered to the threat and within a few minutes were securely bound and gagged. Their horses were located and they were forced to mount them. Their wrists were looped tightly to the saddle horn and their feet were tied beneath the horses' bellies. The horses were then led back down the trail a hundred yards, and Megan and Joe were left to guard them. Hector and Ben went back to the house.

'I get to do the honours on what I thought was my place,' Ben said impassively and flicked matches into the dark, musty interior of the house. Hector fired off his carbine into the surrounding scrub, then pumped a few more rounds into the log cladding. From a distance, and for the gain of anyone listening, it would characterize a fair gunfight.

18

Shortly after nightfall, Carter Krate and Duff Handy reached the rising ground a mile west of the McGovren house. For an hour, they'd sat their horses, waiting.

'Damn strange,' Krate growled. 'They said to meet here.'

'You hear that?' Handy asked ten minutes later, as the muffled sounds of shooting drifted on the night air.

'Yeah, must be right near the MeGovren place.'

The two men waited a while longer, until they saw tongues of spitting flame and thick smoke piercing the inky blue sky ahead of them.

'Goddamn spoilers have gone an' fired the place, without lettin' us know,' Krate yelled anxiously. 'We're supposed to be lookin' out for the girl. If she gets hurt, Felix will skin us.'

Handy sniffed the air as he rode. 'That ain't the smell o' mesquite,' he rasped. 'What the hell is it?'

The riders tore a way through the pear thickets for the McGovren homestead. The old cabin had been built by Ben's father, was made of green pine that had been hauled from the Sangre de Cristo timberline. But many years under the pear country's blistering sun had dried the timber to matchwood.

The smell of burning drifted in as Krate and Handy turned upwind. The roof of the low structure was gone, and charred beams angled into the sky. A stone chimney rose from the pile of still flaming embers where the timbers of one corner had completely burned away. Krate cursed savagely, and nudged his horse forward. He pulled his rifle from its scabbard, held it ready across the horn of his saddle.

He stopped beside one of the small corrals, put a hand out to grip the top rail. He could just make out the pummelled ground where the McGovrens' few stock horses had milled to get out. For a full minute he listened, but there was no sound other than the crackle of searing wood, then he waved Handy closer to the blackened, smoking ruins.

There was enough light for them to discern the cabin's homespun contents, large and small objects appeared to be strewn around the cabin, with curious indistinguishable black mangled heaps.

'What the hell happened here? Where is everybody?' Krate said, in a hushed, awed tone.

'Yeah, who was with them others you were talkin' about?' Handy asked.

'One of 'em was called Red Mayhill. I don't know any more. I think there was four of 'em,' Krate answered, his voice still slow and strained, 'Felix is goin' to raise Cain over this. What the hell happened?' he repeated.

'They burned the place down, 'cause they weren't up to splittin' the reward. They were cuttin' us out,' Handy replied. 'If this feller Mayhill is still around, he's the one goin' to get skinned when he meets up with young Broome.'

'I wouldn't want to spend much time hopin' you're right,' Krate said.

Like prowling jackals, the two 'punchers stole about the shadows, listening and waiting. Eventually, a grey dawn lifted the night's lid, and daylight revealed the blankets of white ash that covered the house and what was left of its contents. Krate and Handy went closer to the pungent, smouldering, ruin.

'This is where the main door was,' Handy said, distractedly, looking around at the charred debris. 'What in hell's name is *this*?' he asked, poking a blackened remnant with the tip of his rifle barrel.

Krate took a close look, thought for a moment then stared horror-struck at his partner. 'It's burned meat. Leave it, for God's sake.'

'Jeesus, Carter, you don't think. . . ?' Handy started in disgust, looked at the dark mangled heaps around him. 'Do you think it's them? Was that the awful stench?'

'Let's get away from here, an' keep your mouth shut,' Krate directed. 'I'm goin' to be across the border before anyone finds out what happened here.'

But then, both men were stopped in their tracks when Felix Broome's voice rasped out at them. 'You ain't goin' anywhere, an' where's the girl . . . where's Megan?' he yelled. The man's face was haggard, and his eyes were red raw as he staggered forward.

'We don't know. We don't even know what happened,' Krate returned. 'You ain't ever goin' to know who was here.'

'I told you to watch out for her. That's what I was goin' to pay you for,' Felix raged, as he levelled his rifle at Krate. He was viciously levering a shell into the chamber, when two co-ordinated shots rang out. One bullet caught him high in the chest, another took Krate in the neck. Neither man uttered a sound as they crashed to the filthy, ash-strewn dirt. Krate rolled onto his back and made an attempt to raise his hands, then they both died staring bewilderedly at each other.

Terrified, Handy was already on the run. He was gasping,

sobbing with fear as he fled from the menacing devastation. His head whirled with thoughts of what had happened and what could happen next. Frightened to near hysteria, he made it to his horse and flung himself up into the saddle. He kicked madly, sought immediate obscurity in the wildness of the pear.

Ben McGovren's procession were well along the trail that led to Lemmon. It was led by Ben himself who was leading Red Mayhill's horse. Behind him came the other prisoners with their bridles tied to the tail of the horse in front. Next came Joe leading a pack horse, then Megan with Hector bringing up the rear.

It was just about when Handy was poking his rifle at the charred remains of a chunk of quartered calf that the riders came to a halt. The land around them was brightening with the first light, and Ben pointed through the prickly pear to indicate a big, lone oak up ahead of them. Hector nodded that he understood, but Joe asked where they were.

'The Rio Bonito's ahead, then the Standin' K. We're below the trail that runs to Lemmon, not more'n a mile from the ranch house. We'll set camp shortly.'

The riders wound on through the thickets, and just as the sun was picking up they drew rein. It was where the prickly pear broke down, and they decided not to ride into the clearings. The prisoners were dismounted and secured to a taller mesquite. All the horses were unsaddled and a cold camp was set. No one was much in the frame of mind for what remained of the beef and biscuits, so Hector, Joe and Megan shared Ben's crock of Pass whiskey. Each had their own thoughts, but when it sank in that her small number of clothes had been burned, Megan had become silent and morose. All she had in the world now was her duck pants, wool shirt, boots, and a battered Stetson.

'I was thinkin' what you said about one o' these turkeys bein' Wilshaw Broome,' Hec said. 'We could have had us our own a little neck-tie party.'

'Still can,' Ben agreed, but turned to Joe. 'What do you want do?' he asked. 'Here's the chance to claim your part o' the fight.'

'Yeah, only trouble bein' I'm a tad lost,' Joe responded. 'Not knowin' this rough country, I wouldn't be claimin' anythin' for long.'

'No issues with that, Joe,' Hec said. 'Me an' Ben'll take care o' the trails an' hidin' places. You just got to say what you want done next. An' remember, it was Broome's orders that sent this family o' rats to burn us all alive.'

'I ain't likely to forget that,' Joe replied. 'But I already decided that we don't kill him. Not by shootin' or hangin' or any other way you think up.'

'Why?'

'Because it wouldn't help us or our cause. You know I want the courts to handle this.'

'Bit late for that,' Hector mused. 'I don't see much of a way other than rubbin' him out.'

'That's the old way, Hec. An' if we do, we'll never get it straight,' Joe reasoned. 'Think about it. Broome's riders won't be scared off as long as he's payin' big money for our hides. But if we continue to play on their nerves, they'll weaken. When they find men who've paid the final price, his bounty money won't seem so easy won. They'll get worried an' start quittin'. That'll be the time to take him.'

'The kid might be right, Hec,' Ben said, a touch grudgingly. 'That schoolin's got him talkin' like a lawyer or a preacher, but it makes sense. We've got to get Broome where the wool's short. I know one or two things that'll make him squeal, if we face him with 'em. But not right now.'

'All right,' Hector conceded. 'Just seems we come a long way for cheek turnin'. I knew I shoulda killed him twenty years ago,' he added with obvious spleen.

19

Gripped by the devils of fear, Duff Handy spurred his horse cruelly towards the home pasture of the Standing K ranch. He guessed that Red Mayhill and the others would have told about Ben McGovren's death along with his family and friends, but Handy had a gruesome chapter to add to the story.

It was mid morning when he crossed the home pasture and pulled his exhausted horse up in the yard of the ranch house. Wilshaw Broome was sitting at the top of the broad steps. He'd been waiting impatiently for news, as if his heavy jaws were bit hard into the land.

'Whose ghost you seen?' he snarled before Handy had a chance to speak.

'That ain't funny, boss,' Handy slurred. 'Is Mayhill back yet? Him an' the others?' he asked as he slipped unsteadily from his horse.

'No, no one's back yet. Why?'

'They burned down the McGovren place,' Handy blurted out, paying no heed to Krate's warning. 'There could o' been five or six of 'em in there.'

Broome shook his head slow and thoughtful. 'Whatever you saw, I doubt it's what happened,' he said with a strange, quiet certainty. 'Did you see 'em burn the house, set a flame to it?'

'No, not as such, but—'

'Tell me what you *did* see?' Broome rapped back at him, stepped forward and held out a dipper.

Handy gulped the water. 'I was tellin' you, boss,' he started. 'Krate an' me got to the risin' ground after dark, but nobody else did.'

Broome waited for Handy to drink more water, then he listened unbelievingly for five minutes while the man continued the grisly tale.

'There's somethin' wrong with this story,' Broome growled. 'Where is Krate?'

'I'm gettin' there, boss, but I'm losin' the difference between what did and what didn't happen. God help me, I ain't told you everythin' yet.'

'Then get on with it.'

Handy nodded unsurely 'Felix told Krate yesterday mornin' we was to look out for Megan when the house was burnt. But while we was there lookin' at everythin' just smokin', he comes up. He was real messed up, boss. I don't know what had happened.'

'Felix was there . . . at the cabin?' Broome rasped.

'Yessir. I guess he was lookin' for Megan.' Handy drained the dipper. 'When he saw what had happened, he cursed Krate. He was set to shoot him, an' would have.'

'What do you mean *would have*? What happened?'

'They got shot, both of 'em, didn't stand a chance. Someone was layin' for us.'

'Are you sayin' they're dead? My Felix, too?'

'Yessir.'

Wilshaw Broome's heavy jaw continued to grind and his eyes turned glassy hard. 'Get that horse taken care of,' he rasped, seeing the poor condition of Handy's mount. 'An' get one saddled for me. Are their horses still out there?'

'Yessir, somewhere.'

'We got to get 'em back. We don't want no one else to find 'em.'

Handy nodded his understanding. 'I think that was one o' Krate's concerns, boss,' he said, before turning away.

It was late afternoon when Handy and Broome returned to the ranch with the bodies.

'If anybody asks questions, we found 'em both in the brush. *That's* where they got shot dead,' Broome said as they crossed the yard.

A few of the ranch hands had come in when they got there, but Red Mayhill and his companions weren't among them. The two bodies were laid out and Broome asked for two graves to be dug. They would be out at the burying orchard, a quarter-mile west of the house. There were many sleeping there, most of them having met violent deaths. In fact, all except old Hoope Kettle and three of the women-folk.

Wilshaw Broome would ride out there on his own, later. He was currently thinking that there were many local people, him included, who thought that up to now lives were expendable, deaths were a by-product of hard and dangerous lives. But now his own son had been shot dead, things were suddenly significant and personal.

'We ain't stayin',' he said to Handy. 'I got business in town, an' I want you with me.'

At the wood yard in Lemmon, Wilshaw Broome ordered two coffins to be made and sent out to the Standing K. Then with Handy, he went on to George Daggert's office. As he half expected, the lawyer had Brent Perser with him.

'Glad to find you here,' Broome said, the moment Handy had closed the door behind them. 'You can burn that goddamn paper, now.'

103

'Why would I do that, nothin's changed?' the town clerk asked, with an apparent lack of concern.

Broome smiled icily. 'Except those concerned are dead. McGovren's house got burned last night. Duff here was ridin' up that way. Tell 'em what you saw, Duff,' he egged his man.

Handy nodded halfheartedly. 'There was a heap o' bodies there,' he started reluctantly. 'I'd say five, but they was burned up real bad. There was nothin' anybody could've done.'

'An' we couldn't expect you to carry out a post-mortem, could we?' Broome said, and continued with his own story-line. 'Felix and Carter Krate didn't come in last night, so Duff rode out again an' found 'em in the brush where they'd been shot dead. That would've been late yesterday, an' you don't need to ask who'd be responsible for it. Maybe what happened was heads-up reckonin'. It's too bad about the women, even if they was sodbusters. But Felix is my son.'

'Who are the women?' Daggert asked, after a moment's thought.

'McGovren's wife an' their daughter, Megan.'

'Are you sure o' that?' Perser asked directly.

'Of course it's them. We know who must've been holed up there.'

Perser shared a puzzled glance with Daggert. 'I saw Aileen McGovren here in town, less than an hour ago,' he said.

'The hell you did,' Broome snorted.

Perser raised his chin sharply. 'Well, it certainly weren't no dressmaker's dummy standin' out there on the board-walk,' he replied with dismissive smirk. 'So, I'll just keep them papers until you work up a better story, or produce the evidence.'

'The only goddamn evidence I can produce is a cartload

o' meat cinders. You just been told,' Broome seethed.

'Yeah, an' I just told *you*, I'll get rid o' the papers when there's no one can serve 'em,' Perser retorted. 'Now leave us, we got other business.'

'You'll have *no* business after the next election,' Broome threatened. 'Let's get out o' here,' he said to Handy and threw George Daggert's office door wide, flung the lawyer an irate glare before stomping into the street.

'What do you reckon made Perser say he'd seen the McGovren woman, boss?' Handy asked Broome, five minutes later.

'I been wonderin' that,' Broome said, and jerked roughly on his reins. 'Either he's runnin' scared, or he wants me to pay him somethin' extra to get rid o' what Kettle's got filed. Goddamnit, him an' Daggert's been succourin' off me for years.'

'Well, it gives me the creeps. Last time I saw her, she weren't gettin' ready to go to town, no sir.'

'Forget it,' Broome rasped. 'You ain't goin' to see her or any o' them gun toters again.'

The two riders spurred on in the direction of the ranch. Every now and again, Duff Handy took a nervous glance back over his shoulder.

'What the hell, do you suppose made him patch up a story like that?' Perser asked the lawyer, when Handy and Broome were gone. 'You know he lied.'

'Yeah, I know it,' Daggert said. 'When Wilshaw Broome lies, it's sort o' comfortin'. As comfortin' as fact. His good lie was findin' his boy an' Krate.'

'I wondered why you weren't too grief-stricken. So, you don't think it was them?' Perser asked.

Daggert shook his head. 'Not where they said, it weren't. They more'n likely went to burn down the McGovren house, but got gunned down for their pains. An' that's where Handy might have found 'em. He weren't lying about the place bein' burned, an' I'm satisfied as to who gave the orders. I thought they'd both come apart when you said you'd seen the McGovren woman.'

'I *had* seen her.'

'McGovren's wife? You sayin' she *is* here in town?'

'Yeah, with not so much as a burned finger.'

'Ah well, whether it was her or not, it don't amount to a hill o' beans. Not in the overall scheme o' things.'

'What are you thinkin'?' Perser wanted to know.

'One week ago, the whole matter of a clear title to that land was simply a case of waitin' thirty days. It's Thanksgivin', or thereabouts, until the limitation runs out. But the papers from young Joe Kettle change everythin'.'

'It ain't my expertise, so how? What can be done?' Perser said.

'Broome ought to have compromised with the Kettle boy. He should've taken Judd Kettle's half of the land under the quit-claim,' the lawyer explained. 'You know what they say about a bird in the hand? Because if that case comes up for trial, there's not a chance that he'll get *more* than half under the law, because Judd only *owned* half. Furthermore, there'll be one or two questions that if you an' me answer, we'll be buyin' tickets direct to the pen, as you well know.'

'So why didn't you tell that to Broome?'

Daggert laughed. 'Because he ain't the sort o' man who'll listen if you ain't tellin' him what he wants to hear. He ain't reasonable, ain't known for his debatin' qualities. As soon as the law of limitation was passed he thought his troubles were over, until McGovren started nosin' around.'

'How *did* you help him?' Perser asked.

'I told him to buy McGovren. He said he tried, but got

short shrift. Huh, makes you think the old feller's got more sand than all of us put together. Anyway, I told Broome it was worth payin' for, but he said he wasn't givin' half a lifetime's earnin's to a sodbuster. That was about it.'

'Maybe he's started to regret it.'

'Not if he thinks McGovren, Kettle an' Chaf have been hard baked in that house.'

Daggert looked duly offended at Perser's crude remark. 'If that cabin was burned last night, Mrs McGovren must have come to town some time yesterday,' he suggested. 'So, she was here last night, been here all day today.'

'Yeah, so what the hell's she up to?'

'Wives generally know what their menfolk are up to, but it don't always work the other way round,' Daggert continued.

'How'd you mean?'

'If Aileen McGovren's got an ounce o' shrewd to her, she'll hold herself together on the money her old man turned down. An' she don't have to go home to hear the news.'

Perser nodded. 'Yeah, maybe,' he agreed. 'I heard they'd got well past the love-bird stage.'

'Well, she's safe enough as long as she stays near Lemmon, but that can't make Broome too happy,' Daggert reasoned.

'It sure don't sound like he's goin' to have it *all* his own way,' Perser said. 'If only Hoope Kettle had left a will, eh? I don't know what might or might not have happened at the McGovren place. But I know it couldn't have been easy to get the better o' McGovren an' Hector Chaf. The heir apparent wasn't there just to sign his name, either.'

'Yeah, I agree,' he said, and sighed deeply. 'My view is that you an' me are just about as far into the molasses barrel as we dare get. We'd better start to look as though things are normal, attend to the "other business" you mentioned to Broome. If I was *him*, I'd lower myself down a very deep well.'

20

Joe Kettle handed out tepid canteen water to the prisoners. None of them said a word, except Red Mayhill.

'What you aimin' to do with us?' he asked.

'You were goin' to burn Mr McGovren's house when we caught you,' Joe answered. 'Don't that tell you snmethin'?'

'Yeah, tells us we should've got our work orders a mite sooner.'

'You weren't *workin'*, you brainless scum,' Joe rapped back. 'You was helpin' to slaughter innocent folk in their beds.'

'I ain't sayin' any more.'

Hector walked up to Mayhill. 'Tell us *whose* orders they were,' he said. 'Try lessenin' your guilt by spreadin' the blame around.'

'You won't do anythin' to us, 'cause if you do, Broome will string all o' you across the same tree,' Mayhill sneered.

'Now there's an idea,' Hector threatened, then indicated that they should bind the prisoners up again. 'An' wring the knots an inch,' he added irritably.

An hour before dusk, the prisoners were forced to mount their horses. Ben McGovren went over to where his daughter still lay quietly on her blankets.

'Megan, we got to ride out, but we won't be gone long,' he said. 'Get your horse saddled up, an' be ready to move out when we come back. Are you all right?'

'If I didn't have a heart or a brain, I might be. Where are you goin'?'

'I told you, a short ride, an' that's all you need to know. Now shake yourself.'

Wilshaw Broome and Duff Handy were riding back to the ranch. It was nearly dusk when they reached the Rio Bonito, half a mile from the house. At that point the trail passed through a grove of live oaks. It was an eerie place in the flat dark, and Handy's nerves were already taut. He yelled a curse when Broome's horse suddenly snorted its displeasure and pulled up sharply.

'Jesus, boss,' he croaked in alarm. 'What the hell's happened here?'

Broome had already gulped in a great draught of air at seeing two figures in front of them. The bodies were hanging, strung across the trail with their feet barely clearing the ground. One of them was his straw boss, Red Mayhill, the other looked like one of the men who'd been paid to ambush Ben McGovren. From where their earlobes had been neatly cut off, blood had trickled to the necks of their stained hickory shirts.

'Whoever done this, knew I'd be comin' through here.' Broome felt the cold run of sweat between his shoulder blades. 'By the look of 'em, they ain't been here long,' he said hoarsely. Then he knew for sure who the perpetrators were, and a sudden dread gripped at his vitals. 'Let's get out o' here,' he gasped and stared guardedly into the oaks. 'They'll be found come mornin'.'

Handy had had enough of dead men for one day, so, with only a grunted response, he spurred his horse away from the oak towards the river.

*

Night settled over the gloomy Standing K ranch. Wilshaw Broome sat in his high, beam-ceilinged den, and Handy sat the other side of the broad hearth. Handy hadn't been out of Broome's sight since making his report that morning. Now, as the firelight flickered across Broome's downcast features, he assumed a nervy companionship. But he knew different. His boss wanted him there because he didn't want him talking to anyone else.

Broome sat in wretched silence, He knew the rough country as few others knew it, yet he knew there were places he'd never seen, perhaps where his enemies were now hiding. To Felix and a few others, he'd passed the word to bring down Ben McGovren. Instead, Felix was dead, and there were others who still hadn't showed at the ranch. Maybe they were all somewhere out in the brush, the vultures and coyotes taking turns to tear the bodies apart. He felt almost overpowered by anguish as he summed up his situation. And it couldn't go on. The overall price was now too high, he had to finish it once and for all. Come morning, when the bodies were found, he'd have one hell of an excuse to hunt down the killers of his men. 'Why the hell didn't you stay away?' he yelled.

Throughout the night, Broome went on with his scheming, his avenging. From time to time he tossed a log to the fire, while an emotionally exhausted Handy took a fitful sleep. He was also mindful of keeping watch with the dead, so he made a few lone visits to the two coffins that were in another room. The troubled man could still go for many nights with little rest, but the irony was that *now* he couldn't sleep even if he wanted too, his mind churning with ifs and buts, maybes and certainties.

It was first light when Broome heard a commotion from the ranch-house's yard. He called for Handy to rouse himself, grabbed a shotgun from a rack and went outside. The line rider who had gone out early to check on the remuda had come storming in. He was sitting his horse making garbled noises in an effort to say something.

'Christ, feller, you look like you got the hounds o' hell behind you,' Broome rasped, although he knew the cause of the rider's distress, or thought he did.

'They're out there somewhere, boss,' the man said, catching his breath. 'I went out after the broncs at first light . . . found 'em on the other side of the creek. They struck the trail an' run towards the ranch, but when they reached the crossin', they bolted . . . turned away from the timber.'

Broome stared hard at his rider. 'Why? What happened? he said, now convinced of the answer.

'It was Red an' the others. If it weren't for their shirts an' pants, I wouldn'ta recognized 'em. I think one of 'em was the Mex, Buscar.' The man looked at Broome horrified. 'I'm tellin' you, boss, they was hangin' there in the oaks like fat catkins, an' they'd all got one eat half hacked away.'

But what the rider said wasn't quite what Broome expected, and he held up his hand. 'Hold it. What do you mean, "the others"? How many of 'em were there?' he demanded.

'Four. There was four of 'em. Their mounts were line-hobbled back in the thickets.'

Broome had agreed with Handy that they should be surprised and shocked. Suddenly he had no difficulty in showing that. There were two men hanging when he and Handy came to the timber. That meant the hangmen must have been there at the time, in hiding until they'd passed by. Now, with his worst suspicions come true, his excuse for hunting them down, for giving no quarter was that much greater.

Instead of two, six men were buried that day on Standing

K land, although some burials were a short distance from close friends and family members. After a terse ceremony, Broome gave his orders for the day. His story was that a gang of violent, determined rustlers had re-emerged, that it was no doubt *they* who had hanged and killed Felix and the others. It was obvious their intention was to terrorize Rio Bonito country, make a fast sweep of the range and its cattle. It was up to Broome's remaining men to find and punish them. There'd be no reprieve or stays of execution, just a big dollar bounty for the man or men who destroyed them.

In less than an hour after the last shovelful of earth topped out the graves, a dozen men rode to different stations of the ranch. But Duff Handy wasn't with them. He was the sole survivor of those who'd been delegated to burn the McGovren house, and. Broome wanted him within range, not adding mud to the already very dangerous waters. Thinking on Brent Perser's claim about Aileen McGovren being in town, Broome got to wondering just who had burned in the cabin. 'We know who it wasn't, eh, McGovren?' he muttered.

21

When Hector, Ben and Joe returned, Megan was already on
her horse. She had a fair idea of what had become of Red
Mayhill and his partners, but said nothing. Now they were
riding to find cover from Wilshaw Broome and what was left
of his gang. Joe took the lead rope of the pack pony from
her hand and she fell in behind Ben. Joe followed, and
Hector brought up the rear as usual.

They bent around, sometimes through cactus thickets,
occasionally splashed across shallow fords of the Rio Bonito.
Ben led on through a wilderness of pear, followed every
point of the compass in their winding flight. Joe estimated
that they were taking two or three miles to gain one in
making it to the lone oak they had seen in the early morning.

It was long past midnight when they rode into a pocket
of what appeared to be an impenetrable barrier of prickly
pear. Ben stopped, spoke for the first time in two hours.

'Close up,' he said, 'it's easier to make a trail.' Then he
moved on, twitching left and right, scraping his legs
through the harsh, unyielding vegetation.

Joe was unhappy at the thought of taking flight before
Wilshaw Broome. And he was thinking of the hanged men,
the trademark, ear-cropping of Hector Chaf. He didn't

know then that the disfigurement had a peculiar signifi-
cance to Broome, that it was a personal matter between the
two men. Joe was sickened at the feral cruelty, but he understood the country's ruthless nature and the men who lived
by way of it. He also knew that in the end, he could be living
or dying by it himself. Through listening to Ben and Hector,
he was convinced that if there was but a single man working
for Broome who wasn't a lawbreaker, it was because Broome
didn't know it. Broome's personnel were the kind of men
who'd usurped the loyalties of Hector Chaf and Ben
McGovren, and Joe was now certain that the land gifted by
his own grandfather was the McGovrens by any reasonable
law. After gaining control from Broome, it would be once
again, he concluded.

Joe's mind was still agitated when they rode into a wide
clearing. He hauled in his mount, saw the lone oak tree
against the lightening sky.

'You know this place?' Ben asked Hector.

'Yeah, I do. But the pear's bigger and taller than it used
to be. Ol' Cochise himself might have difficulty findin' us in
here.'

'Good, let's camp,' Ben said.

They all dismounted a little way from the tree, quietly
unsaddled and line-hobbled their horses to graze. Still without a word, each one of them then rolled themselves into
their blankets. Within minutes, and due mainly to the
torment of weariness and nervous tension, they were sound
asleep.

When Joe woke five hours later, he sat up, kicked away
his blankets, rubbed his eyes and cursed. At the other side
of the glade, there were five horses quietly snatching at the
meagre brome. He blinked, cursed again and was about to
shout something, when there was a sharp whistle at the edge
of the thicket. He looked around, saw that Megan was

watching him from a gap in her blanket. Hector propped himself up on his left elbow, raised his carbine with his right hand. Ben put his fingers to his lips and gave a returning whistle.

Emerging from the scrub, an old, stooped man came walking slowly towards them. He had a straggly beard, and his grey hair fell to his shoulders.

'Jeesus,' Hector huffed with astonishment, 'the Apaches' have found us, after all.'

'Come on in, Quedo,' Ben called out. 'Hector's here; you'll remember him.'

'Sure I remember him,' Quedo Lunes replied. 'He's maybe one o' the white men worth rememberin'. An' I'd know him by way he's stacked up . . . even when he's lyin' down. That'll be Mr Jasper rubbin' sleep from his eyes. He ain't aged much like the rest of us . . . must be a clean' livin' one,' Lunes chuckled at his own quip.

Joe got to his feet. He was about to query what the old man meant, but Hector stopped him. 'The crazy galoot don't mean anythin',' he said. 'He's just spent too many years suckin' on mescal. An' in this light, you *could* favour your pa,' he added with a roguish grin.

Megan rolled from her blanket and pushed herself up, stared enquiringly at the wild-looking old man.

'It's all right, Megan,' Ben said. 'This is Quedo Lunes. You've heard me speak of him.'

'Nice-lookin' boy,' Lunes chuckled, then, paying no more attention to any of them, he turned and walked off, told them to follow.

Megan sniffed and pulled her pants belt in a notch. 'I really liked the cabin, an' Ma an' pig an' cow an' horse dirt,' she muttered. 'I knew where I stood.'

Two hours later, they followed Lunes through a gap in the thicket and eventually found themselves in another

116

clearing that was surrounded by old pear and high mesquite. Up tight to the brush were three earth lodges around a shallow water pocket. Another Mexican was sitting cross-legged, rolling up tacos of cold beans and beef.

'It's us, Gitano. We're here,' Lunes called out.

The man looked up, nodded non-committally and spoke rapidly in his own language. '*No la Ciudad*,' he said, which more or less meant that he only expected to see Ben McGovren and Quedo.

'We're all safe, Gitano,' Lunes appeased. 'I've brought Hector Chaf an' Ben. You know them. Mr Jasper an' Ben's *muchachos*, here too.'

Gitano gave a hardly noticeable response and went back to preparing the tacos. Joe looked towards Megan, and winked, smiled understandingly. For himself, he did bear a striking resemblance to his father, and he'd be about the same age as when the two Mexicans had last seen him.

After a supper of sow-belly and biscuits, Gitano, Megan, Joe, Hector and Quedo Lunes sat talking with Ben.

'I ain't told you just what Quedo was bringin' you here for,' he said. 'But I did tell you I had some stuff that would make Wilshaw Broome squeal. An' I didn't mean in any courtroom.'

'What sort o' stuff are you talkin' about, Ben?' Hec asked.

'Quedo,' Ben started. 'He told me Broome hired Gitano an' two another Mexes to kill Judd Kettle.'

Hector looked quickly from Ben to Lunes, back to Ben. 'I thought he fell from his horse an' broke his neck. Too full o' cactus juice, you said.'

'Yeah, I know,' Ben acknowledged. 'But there was others who didn't think that.'

'So what the hell *did* happen?'

'Yeah, how're *these* fellers implicated?' Joe wanted to know.

'Quedo ain't, an' Gitano was only ever used to doin' what Broome told him. It was him an' two others who were paid to bushwhack Judd. A couple o' miles west o' the ranch house, they beat him senseless before puttin' him back up on his horse, an' slappin' it scared towards town. It was a miracle he got that far, I guess. Because he weren't shot, folk just sort o' assumed . . . said he'd been drinkin'. That was the story got put around.'

'So one of 'em's here, what happened to the other two?' Hector asked.

'Next day, Broome shot 'em both . . . threw 'em deep in the pear. Who the hell's goin' to check, let alone care? *No one*, except Gitano, but he knew his way around.'

'Where do *you* come in?' Megan asked Lunes, the wild, old Mexican.

'I was already here,' he said pithily. 'How do you say – "wrong place, wrong time"? It's the story o' my life,' he added with a heartfelt grimace.

'An' how'd *you* find 'em?' Hector asked of Ben.

'I didn't. Gitano got away an' took to this thicket. Not long after, Quedo got tired of actin' the lunatic in Fort Wingate, an' decided to shack up here with him. They been livin' here for years. I'm more or less the only two-legged critter they seen in a long time.'

Joe had been holding something in his mind for a few minutes. 'You've known about Judd for some time, Ben. I know you're *supposed* to say nothin' if you can't say somethin' good about folk, but he was my uncle. Why didn't you tell us, before now?' he asked.

Ben nodded amenably. 'Because I wondered about the worth of it all. I thought about givin' up, an' movin' on. I'd lost my land an' didn't expect to get it back, got tired all of a sudden. It ain't much, but it's sort o' why, Joe, an' I'm sorry. But now you're here, maybe I can suck in another breath. I'll be good an' ready to go with whatever you want.'

Joe smiled. 'Thank you, Ben. An' we'll build you a bigger, better cabin, with a load o' new store boughts,' he promised enthusiastically.

It was near midnight, and Ben was talking family stuff with Megan. Joe had walked off a ways with Hector.

'I want you to have the Standin K, Joe, but not on top o' more graves,' Hector said quietly. 'An' now Ben's gettin' to be as feral as them two Mexes. I just hope it ain't catchin'.'

Joe thought for a moment, shook his head for a suitable response, then came back on another tack. 'It looks like we got ourselves a well-stocked an' sited camp here,' he replied. 'We'll smoke 'em . . . make sure that none o' them graves are ours. Now, I got to go an' see Ben.'

'Hello, young feller,' Ben said, looking up as Joe approached. 'You look like you got somethin' on your mind.'

'Ben, I got to say this, just so's there ain't any misunderstandin' when it's too late.' Joe nodded at Megan. 'Miss Megan here ain't ridin' with us, an' she ain't stayin' in this camp alone neither.'

'An' how do you figure to work that?' Ben asked with a dry smile.

'I ride out with Hec one day, an' you the next. An' whoever's comin' tomorrow, must be ready long before first light. Wherever it is we ride, we don't come anywhere near here, either side o' full dark. We'll use night markers. That's the meat o' what I got to say, an' none of it's negotiable,' Joe answered decisively.

'Huh, straight in, eh, kid. Reminds me o' your gran'pa,' Ben snapped back.

'I'll ride with you first. An' *that* ain't negotiable either,'

119

Hec added.

'Sounds like *I* don't have much to negotiate *with*,' Megan muttered sarcastically.

22

Joe and Hector were riding a low hogback. They were surrounded by open country, mesquite that stretched into the distance.

'Just in case you have to go home alone, Joe, I suggest you take a look back,' Hector said, drawing in his mount. 'You see that ol' oak of ours?'

'Yeah, the one looks like there's some sort o' hawk sittin' on a top branch,' Joe observed.

'That's it. Well, that's five miles. So it's near ten to the centre of Standin' K. It's six miles east to the Rio Bonito, an' the same distance beyond that's range land. There's some real big spreads out there, but they keep most o' their cattle in with a drift line. They know better than to lose 'em out here. That leaves Mr Wilshaw Broome with his own private bear garden.'

'Why *did* my great gran'father ever settle here?'

'To get the Rio Bonito. Before they knew much about wells an' win'mills, water was as scarce as women in the open country west o' here. But put some moisture into it, an' it's good, productive range,' Hec explained. 'Now, let's get a bearin' on things,' he said. 'Lookin' from here to camp, there's a group o' trees right in line with the lone oak. Get yourself a fix on that, an' now look north. You see a stand o' timber, and another, beyond that?'

'Yeah, I've got 'em,' Joe said.

'Well, If you lose your way, those landmarks will steer you back to camp. Broome's men will be comin' from that direction to look for us. What he don't know is, we're smokin' *them* out. So, young Joe, that's where we're headed.'

'A man surprised is half beaten, eh, Hec?' Joe suggested.

'Yeah, let's hope. I think if I'd known what was in line for us, I wouldn't have shown you Ben's letter,' Hec confessed. 'Broome will have discovered his gunnies with my earmark taggin' an' figure we ain't ended up as skillet pork. The only thing he'll be doin' now, is issuin' lead.'

'If you're givin' me a chance to climb into a gopher hole, Hec, you ain't succeedin'. As far as I'm concerned, the sooner we have our little gunfight, the better.'

It was far into the day, and they were crossing an open stretch of mesquite. They were close to the timber stand when the first shot cracked out. Hector cursed, kick-heeled his horse and swerved to the cover of the oaks. Joe pushed in alongside him as three more quick shots reverberated across the scrubland.

'Jeeesus, Hec, it looks like I got my wish,' Joe shouted.

'Either that, or them gophers are packin' pistols,' he quipped.

'We sure got someone disturbed,' Hec grated. 'That was a signal. Probably for anyone that's close to come an' help. Well, if they do, we know from where they'll be comin'. We'll tie-in the horses, take 'em on foot an' use our carbines.'

Joe and Hector securely tethered their mounts deeper into the timber, then edged back to position themselves either side of one of the perimeter oaks.

'As long as they stay in front of us, we've got the drop,' Hec said, and calmly levered a shell into his carbine. 'If they do come, we destroy 'em, even if they turn an' run. Be a goddamn turkey shoot.'

Less than a minute later, they heard a rumble of hoofs just beyond the stretch of open ground.

'It sounds like they're comin' from both sides,' Joe said. 'I don't believe it, Hec, we got us a flank each.'

Hector gave a short salute with his left hand. 'Yessir,' he said, 'but maybe we should start wonderin' how many there are.'

From across the scrub clearing, a head showed above the shoulder-high mesquite and prickly pear. Joe's carbine immediately cracked out and Hector grunted, fired two shots into the echo.

'They're comin' through,' Hec yelled.

By a careful and considered pattern of fire, Hector and Joe levelled a deady fusillade as the riders came at them. Only one rider of four made it into the clearing after breaking from cover. He reined his horse, fired just one shot, as another of Joe's bullets hit him low in the front.

'Hell, Joe, where'd you learn to shoot like that?' Hector rasped.

'Westwater Bend, an' *you* taught me,' Joe replied without a moment's thought.

'Hmm, well, I don't know where Broome bought these gunnies, but I guess they weren't earnin' top rate,' Hector added.

'Maybe their horses are worth more. We should go get 'em,' Joe suggested.

'The one out front ain't dead yet. He might be savin' a bullet for one of us,' Hector said. 'An' we still don't know how many there were.'

'I'll wager that was all of 'em.' With that, Joe walked purposefully across the open scrub.

The stricken man had regained some awareness. He looked around for his horse, asked for water as Joe approached.

'You know water ain't good for a feller who's gut shot,' Joe said. 'There ain't nothin' we can do for you.'

'You never gave us a chance, openin' up like that,' the man uttered in a despairing croak.

'Oh yeah, an' four against two's your idea o' fair odds, is it?' Joe said dismissively.

'You shoulda thought about dyin' before you took Broome's coin,' Hector added curtly.

'I'll get their horses,' Joe said. 'Just don't kill him.'

The four horses were standing nearby. They had attempted a meagre graze almost instantly, oblivious to the noise of the gunfire. 'Must be used to it, I guess,' Joe muttered, and led them back to where him and Hector had brought their riders down. They turned a rope around each of the dead men's shoulders and under the arms, then dragged the three of them into the brush. Finally, Hector drew a folding knife from his pants pocket.

'I'll see to the other feller,' Joe said and turned away. Single-handed, he eased the man to his feet and hauled him up and into the saddle. Then he tied the man's hands, lashed his ankles tight beneath the belly of his horse.

'An' you've got your boots on,' Joe said after giving the fellow a drink from his canteen. 'Life ain't so bad.'

'Yeah, thanks, Copper,' the confused, bedevilled man spluttered and coughed painfully.

'No thanks needed,' Flee said, leading the other horses. 'In five minutes, you'll be wishin' we'd left you to die *here*.'

The four horses now caught the cloying scent of blood and they crow-hopped, snorted uneasily. Hec slapped them on their rumps, shouted as they tore off through the brush.

'Even if they make it back to where they come from, it'll make no difference to what Broome wants,' Hec said, after a moment's weighing up of the situation. 'Besides, there's

Ben to think of. He'll want his share o' the reckonin'. Lunes too, maybe.'

Without saying much more, the two men mounted up and started back to the camp.

'You know what I was sayin' about makin' no difference to Broome,' Hec started, after ten minutes, 'it's because his men are paid to die. He just rubs 'em from his tally sheet. An' I can see your reasonin' about takin' him alive, bringin' all his sins into the open. But we'll have to confront him with Lunes and Gitano, an' that won't be easy.'

It was nearing midnight when they entered their camp. Ben and Megan were standing beside one of the lodges, the tension easing only when they let the barrels of their guns drop.

Gitano emerged from the shadows and took a bowl of warm posole from one of the clay ovens. Ben started pouring coffee, while Megan stared pensively at Joe. Once again, she caught herself comparing him to Felix Broome. Not yet knowing of his fate, she nodded unhappily at Joe, ducked her head as she edged into the darkness of her lodge. Whatever the differences between Joe and Felix, it didn't alter the fact that it was Felix who'd said he wanted her for his wife.

23

Out at the Standing K, three riderless horses came racing into the ranch-house yard. A few minutes later, a small group of men untied a man from the saddle of a fourth horse. In the spread of yellow light from the bunkhouse lamps, one of them called out to Wilshaw Broome, 'It's Max Pepper. Looks like he's still alive.'

Broome was sitting in the deep shadows of the house veranda. 'Get him down an' into the bunkhouse,' he shouted back.

The gravely wounded man was put on a cot, and one of the 'punchers took a closer look at the man's belly wound. 'This sort o' hurt don't give you too long,' he declared pessimistically.

'Let me talk to him,' Broome said. 'Who shot you, Max? Where'd it happen?' he asked with little consideration for the man's suffering.

'One o' the timber stands,' the man choked out.

'Who was it tied you to your mount?'

'Copper. It was Copper helped me . . . couldn't see too clear.'

'So, who shot you? Where are the others?' Broome demanded to know.

'It was the devil himself come out o' the flames, Mr Broome. I seen him up close.'

'What do you mean, "the devil"? Who did you see?'

But Max Pepper didn't answer. He rambled on feverishly while the men exchanged worried looks with one another.

'Goddamnit,' Broome cursed impatiently. 'Give him a shot o' liquor.'

'Let me,' Copper Thorpe said, and offered a tin mug to Pepper's lips. The stricken man gulped instinctively, opened his eyes at the effect.

'Is that you, Copper?' he garbled. 'You saw them devils, didn't you?' Pepper closed his eyes, made one attempt to lick his lips, then he died.

'He said there was more'n one devil,' Thorpe said tentatively, and shook his head. 'An' he thinks *I* was there with him. Bein' gut shot ain't the sharpest way to ride brush country.'

'He didn't know who or what he saw. He didn't even know what he was sayin',' Broome snapped. 'We'll cut this nonsense now by some o' you unsaddlin' the horses, an' some o' you takin' care o' Pepper.'

When the horses were turned loose and the saddles hung up, Duff Handy was in no hurry to get back to the house.

'What do you reckon Max meant by seein' devils?' a big-jawed 'puncher called Frog Petty asked him. 'He must've seen somethin'.'

'Yeah, he saw a devil o' sorts, all right,' Handy agreed. 'He just couldn't bring himself to tag a name to it.'

'Maybe it was that ol' Hoope Kettle come back,' Petty suggested, his wide lips quivering. 'From what I heard, he ain't ever far from this place.'

'Listen, Frog, Broome's pittin' you against somethin' you can't kill,' Handy said. Then without waiting for a response he continued quickly, told Petty about the burning of McGovren's cabin, that Brent Perser had seen Aileen McGovren in town. 'You best let some o' the boys know.'

127

'Why ain't you ridin' with the rest of the gang, Duff? Why ain't you tryin' to catch whoever it is we're after?'

'I know too much, an' the old man don't want me out o' his sight,' Handy replied.

'Handy, where the hell are you?' Broome interrupted, with a shout from the bunkhouse door.

'See?' Handy said. He winked at Petty and tapped the side of his nose.

'I told you to stay with me,' Broome continued harshly.

'I'm right here, boss,' Handy answered him. 'When you said to unsaddle the horses, I went right to it.'

'Well, I didn't mean you. I told you to stay away from the hands. Let's get back to the house.'

But the cage door had been opened, and throughout the night, the restless 'punchers sat about the bunkhouse. Each time Duff Handy's tale was told, a little bit was taken away or a little bit added, until they all had the root of a horrifying tale. By first light, more than one rider had made up his mind to quit the Standing K, the demon-hunting payroll of Wilshaw Broome.

After the burial of Max Pepper, Broome was waiting at the main corral. He was ready to issue further commands on the impending manhunt, but it was Frog Petty who got in first.

'Me an' one or two o' the boys are aimin' to collect our pay, Mr Broome,' he said, with as much assurance as he could muster.

'An' why don't that surprise me?' Broome rasped back. 'You an' Handy formin' a whisper club's got nothin' to do with it, I suppose?'

'Rustlers are normally out for beef an' broncs, Mr Broome. That's who you told us we were up against. But now there's wind o' some real spooky stuff happenin', an' it didn't have to be Duff who told us. We're gettin' out before we get brought home like Max,' Petty declared.

'You're yellow,' Broome snarled. 'Yellow an' scared o' your own shadows. Those o' you that want that pay, come by at the end o' the week. Meantime, get your traps from the bunkhouse an' clear the ranch.'

An hour later, Broome was back in the shadows of the house veranda. Knowing there was something final needed, he was silently watching, pondering his next move.

'Hey, Jollife, do *you* get spooked easy?' he called out to a man who was carrying the look of an opportunist.

'No, boss. Never seen much to get me that way,' Tark Jolliffe answered back.

'Good, 'cause the Standin' K's lookin' for a new foreman. You been here long enough to know what's to be done, an' you know how we handle rustlers an' killers. So take whatever men are left an' go get 'em. I'll give each o' you six months' extra pay for them you dispatch. A year's, if you bring 'em in kickin'.'

'That's a darn sight more'n you offered the others,' Jollife muttered. Due to the most recent developments, the man was feeling confident at his new-found status with Wilshaw Broome.

It was shortly after first light when the men rode off. Broome deemed that the men who'd remained were of like feather, big profits distilling them to a hardline. But nearer the truth was, there were few places that such men would find ready employment along the Rio Bonito.

'They'll get results,' Broome said.

'Not if they come up against the likes o' what Max was talkin' about,' Handy answered.

'Yeah, that reminds me, what the hell did you tell Frog Petty?' Broome demanded from Handy.

'Nothin'. I was speculatin' along with the others,' Handy lied. 'It was Max who got the worms in his head.'

'Well I'm goin' to have to decide your future pretty soon, feller, an' promotion sure ain't in the wind,' Broome said ominously.

Handy looked suitably worried, before turning away towards the empty bunkhouse. 'I'll go trim them lamp wicks, afore the place burns down,' he said obligingly. But he was already wondering if Wilshaw Broome had thought everything out. After all, Handy was just about the only man in the outfit who hadn't had his hand in a killing, or the burning of the McGovren cabin. Also, he'd met Megan and liked her. When he'd prodded the charred remains of what Carter Krate said was a body, he'd felt physically sick. Now he didn't know what it was that Broome had in mind for him, and wondered why he hadn't quit with the others.

Throughout the rest of the day, unaware of what was going on in the various parts of the ranch, Handy and Broome kept close to the house. At that stage, Handy wasn't unduly worried because he could keep a distrustful eye on his boss. In fact, on one occasion, he considered putting a bullet or two between the man's shoulder blades. He smiled ruefully, reckoned that even if he stamped the man's forehead with his own initials and ran, he'd be well down the list of likely suspects.

24

'Where's Pa?' Megan asked Hector Chaf, early the following morning.

'He's with Joe. They rode out long before first light,' Hector answered.

'Why? I mean, why did he ride out with Joe?'

'Because, young lady, that was the understandin'. I was to ride with Joe one day, an' Ben the next. "Weren't negotiable", Joe said. That was the price he set. Don't you remember?'

'I remember I didn't get a chance to put in my two cents worth. I would've said that it was a needless danger for two men to ride out there.'

'Well, me an' Joe came back unscathed,' Hector smiled considerately.

'That's how it appeared, but the night couldn't have been much darker. I couldn't see whether you had a fight or not, an' you never mentioned it.'

'Hah, we brushed some flies away. Nothin' worth makin' a fuss over.'

'It's not a lot to ask what's goin' on, if I'm to sit here twiddlin' my thumbs.'

'Yeah, fair enough, Megan,' Hector said. 'After we've ate some o' what ol' Gitano calls breakfast, I'll tell you about it.'

Joe and Ben had ridden north that morning. They had searched around the scene of the previous day's clash, and then beyond the oak stand, but they hadn't seen hide nor hair of a Wilshaw Broome man.

'You fellows must've put some scare into 'em,' Ben said. 'We've raked through the most likely places an' ain't sniffed so much as a rattler's fart. Whoever they are, they're sure happy to give this place a miss,'

'Yeah, well, they done the right thing there,' Joe granted. 'It's gettin' late, so maybe we should think about headin' home.' With that, he positioned them on the landmark line and rode.

The two riders were several miles south of the oak stand. They were crossing a clearing with the sun in their eyes, when Joe heard Ben yell out. In the same instant a rifle shot crashed across the surrounding thicket and Ben pitched from his saddle.

Joe yelled and raced forward to help. He was nearing the far edge of the brush, when Ben got to his feet. Ben looked dizzily around him, then fell again within a few feet of the unforgiving vegetation.

'They ain't given this place a miss, goddamnit,' Joe cursed. 'They've been laid up waitin' for us.' He was making a grab for his carbine, when his horse stumbled. Its legs buckled and its neck arched down as a bullet smashed into its bony forehead. He cursed again, freed the stirrups as the stricken animal collapsed under him, He dived to the ground, let go of his carbine as he rolled clear. He drew his pistol as he heard the sound of hoofs pounding the ground behind him. But he didn't have time to turn or do much else before he was thumped hard from behind, and the world turned black.

When Joe regained consciousness, the sun was sinking towards first dark. He was on his side, lying on the ground with his feet loosely bound, but his wrists and hands were tight. A small group of men stood around him, and the ruthless face of Tark Jollife peered at him, closely.

'He's comin' round,' Wilshaw Broome's new foreman said. 'He ain't messed up, just got the wind knocked from him.'

'As long as he can appreciate the view from a big ol' oak branch,' one of the men said.

'No!' Jollife snapped quickly. 'Boss is payin' double for bringin' 'em in alive.'

As darkness fell, Joe remained very still on the ground. He could hear men cursing at the painful scratch of thorns as they beat about the pear thicket. He thought that if Ben had managed to crawl somewhere to safety, maybe he wasn't that badly wounded, that maybe he was waiting for the opportunity to make a move. When Joe was young and headed off to Tacoma, he recalled Hector was always saying, "May bees never fly at this time o' year". 'Now I know what you meant,' he muttered, and grinned ruefully.

'We can't find the other one,' the man who wanted to hang Joe, said. 'A few scratches ain't much for a couple o' hundred bucks, but it's gettin' real dark in there, an' he might not be plumb dead yet.'

'If he's carryin' a bullet, he won't last long. Let's get back to the ranch, an' we'll come back in the mornin'.' Tark Jollife didn't accept any of Max Pepper's bunkum about devils, but he wasn't going to test it by dallying.

They helped Joe to his feet, untied his ankles and put him up on Ben's horse.

'Don't fall,' Jollife said. 'Mr Broome'll think we ain't been lookin' after you.'

As the group of riders started their journey to the

Standing K ranch, Joe peered into the surrounding darkness, the forbidding tangle of pear and matchweed. Sorry
Ben, weren't such a good idea after all, lettin' *me* say what's
what, he thought to himself. To Joe, it now looked like it was
the end of their fight, and he couldn't help but choke on
his prospects. He'd been hopeful when he'd ridden out
with Hector, and then Ben. But if he'd known about the
dollars that Broome was putting up, maybe he would have
guessed that a handful of men would have the incentive, if
not the stomach, to remain and fight.

Using the lives of others as currency, Wilshaw Broome
had paid a very high price to retain the Standing K.
Consequently, Joe was expecting some of Hector and Ben's
own particular type of medicine in return when they arrived
at the ranch. But maybe Broome would think twice about
harming him with an armed and angry Hector Chaf still
prowling around. Furthermore, he'd promised to build a
bigger, better cabin for the McGovrens.

Hector sat for a long hour staring into the embers of the
fire, mulling stuff over. His eyes and ears were straining to
interpret the sounds of the night, the approach of friend or
foe, but his mind was on something else.

The rest of the state was growing up, folk were changing
with the times, getting civilized. But along the Rio Bonito,
out on the Standing K, men still held a fundamentally cruel
and primal outlook. The fight he was involved in gave both
good and evil leanings of men full sway. It was where might
prevailed and, right now, that was Wilshaw Broome and his
outfit.

With midnight far gone, no news of Joe and Ben was
more than he could endure. He wanted to be out there
looking for them, but Joe had told Ben that Megan should
not be left there with only Gitano and Lunes, and he had

agreed. He cursed quiet exasperation, eased himself to his feet and walked over to the higher sided slope of Megan's lodge.

'Megan,' he called softly.

A very short moment later, Megan stepped out. 'Have Pa and Joe come in yet?' she asked.

'No,' Hector answered. 'Megan, you know you're supposed to stay here, an' I'm to watch over you, no matter what?'

'Yeah, I know. Why?'

'I ain't been thinkin' much else other than about Ben and Joe. I know you have too, no sense pretendin' otherwise.'

'I know what you're thinkin' of, Hector Chaf, an' before you say whatever it is you're goin' to say, I'm dressed an' ready to ride with you. No negotiatin',' Megan declared.

The pair of them took a narrow channel in the pear, quietly stole to the big old oak where their saddles and horses were. Within five minutes they were mounted, and guided by the stars, started on a northwards trail.

Every few minutes, Hector held up their ride. He stopped, drew his Colt revolver and cocked the trigger. The swift, sharp sound breached the still night, and he stopped to listen before riding on again. It was a few miles before they got close to where Joe and Ben had been bushwhacked and Joe pulled his gun once again. The ominous metallic click penetrated the surrounding brush, but this time Hector raised his hand for Megan to halt alongside him.

He pointed his Colt off to their left, waited a moment until they heard a low rumbling cough from the edge of the thicket.

'At a time like this, you're the only one dumb enough to try that ol' signal, Hec,' Ben groaned out. 'My leg's hurt bad.'

Hector and Megan were quickly on the ground and

making a run to where Ben was laying up.

'Leg took a bullet, but it's nothin' that a glug o' my patent medicine won't cure,' he gasped. 'What took you so long?'

'You'll be OK now, Pa, but where's Joe?' Megan asked.

'Yeah, I heard 'em. But I was holed up with a family o' cottontails. Them fellers are real schooled in the ways o' bein' hush scared.'

Hector rode back to camp with Ben riding in front of him. Megan followed. She was distressed and very tired, but she kept her senses alert for anything other than the sounds of disturbed critters and the sigh of night breezes.

Dawn was breaking when they reached camp. Using their own mixture of nature's remedies, Gitano and Lunes worked on Ben's leg. As they cleansed the wound and stopped the flow of blood, Hector set the Pass whiskey crock to Ben's lips. The wounded man took a swallow, grimaced and spat painfully.

'What in hell's name's that?' he rasped and opened his watering eyes.

'You tell me, you ol' goat. You probably been drinkin' it since you were knee-high to a grasshopper,' Hector chided.

'So where would they go? Where would they have taken Joe?' Megan persisted nervously.

'I heard one of 'em say somethin', then someone else said they were gettin' back to the ranch for Broome to have *his* say.' Ben then twisted his head towards Hector. 'If they *have* got him, he might've been better out there in the prickly,' he said.

Hector shook his head slowly. 'Not if I have it my way,' he threatened.

Gitano, who'd been kneeling close, suddenly rose to his feet and backed off. He grabbed his long-barrelled gun and walked quickly to the edge of the small clearing. Without saying a word, Quedo Lunes was close on his heels.

'I thought *my* faculties were still sharp, but them ol' Mexes got the ears o' bats. There's somebody comin', Megan, so look to your pa,' Hector said.

25

It was well after nightfall when Tark Jollife and his men reached the Standing K ranch house. With Duff Handy alongside him, Wilshaw Broome hurriedly crossed the yard to meet them.

'Who you go there?' Broome called out.

'One o' your rustlers, an' he's alive,' Jollife replied. 'But he ain't said much.'

'How many of 'em were there?' Broome demanded.

'Him an' one other. He crawled off to die, we reckon. We'll go find his carcass in the mornin' . . . bring him in if there's anythin' left.'

'You won't leave anythin' to the mornin,' Broome called out. 'Bring him into the house, get some food, then go find the other one. Thinkin' these men are dead's cost me dear.'

Two men pulled Joe from his horse, and with Jollife on one side and a burly 'puncher on the other, he was led into the house and through to Broome's den. On the way, Joe cast an incensed eye at the house and its trappings. Mine, he thought, then mindful of his predicament, changed his mind.

'Put him in that chair,' Broome ordered.

Joe wasn't to know it, but it was the same chair that his father and uncle had often sat in many years before when it was the Kettles' inner sanctum.

Under the broad, hanging cluster of lamps, Broome suddenly looked closer at Joe, his eyes squinting inquisitively.

'You keep him covered, Handy, an' get his feet tied,' he said. 'Tark, your money's all here, plus a bonus if an' when you bring the other one back. Go now an' take a couple o' men with you.' Then he again looked closely at Joe's features. 'Have we met before?' he asked.

'You met my pa,' Joe answered back. 'I'm told there's a passin' resemblance.'

'An' who'd he be?'

'Kettle. Jasper Kettle,' Joe said firmly. 'It ain't the way I had it planned, but I've come home.'

Broome's usual high colour faded, and his jaw worked nervously. He was facing something implausible, something that by all reckoning, just couldn't be.

'Joe Kettle died with Hector Chaf an' Ben McGovren. They was there when the McGovren place burned down,' he offered, trying for a grip on reality.

Joe raised a weary smile. 'Hardly. You got eyes,' he said icily.

'So who the hell was out there with you in the pear?' he asked, dreading the reply.

'Ben McGovren,' Joe confirmed. 'An' before that brain o' yours makes its flyblown mind up, Hector Chaf's still out there, too. There's someone with many years o' bad feelin' against you, Broome, so you got a problem. At least one of 'em's comin' to get you.'

As his words chewed up Broome, Joe saw the overwhelming effect they were having on Duff Handy. The man was so scared that his tension-gripped pistol had fallen away until it was pointing down at the polished floor.

'Who do you think's been shootin' your men?' Joe continued. 'Fireflies?'

139

As Broome recoiled from the implications, Joe knew that he'd likely only get one chance before the man struck out. It would be an irrational response, out of wild fear, and just about in place.

Joe grunted, roared with defiance and cannoned himself up and out of the chair. In one pistoned blow he caught Broom in his mouth, tight and very hard up under his nose. A bone cracked and gave way, and Broome went reeling backwards into an insensible heap.

Handy stood frozen, as Joe suspected he would, and he turned to face him as he stripped the rope from around his ankles.

'Fire that thing, mister, an' I'll get my hounds to follow you for ever,' he rasped out, smiled coldly at the worth of his threat. 'But help me, an' we'll both get away from here, if that's what you want.'

'Yeah, I'm comin' with you,' Handy agreed.

'You don't speak unless spoken to, an' then everythin's just fine,' Joe said, pulling Broome's Colt from its holster.

The two men stole from the house and on to the corral. They rapidly saddled two horses and turned at a gallop down the Rio Bonito. They rode fast for half a mile, then Joe turned west. They were soon off the range land and into the pear thickets where they reined in.

'Somethin's been botherin' me, mister,' Joe said. 'Other than you think I'm some sort o' hell-hound, why didn't you shoot me back there when you had the chance? Broome would've been payin' you to do just that.'

'Because of what I know,' Handy replied. 'Whatever he had in mind for you, sooner or later it would've been the same for me.'

'Well, your chances ain't much improved,' Joe suggested. 'Now you got to tell me what you know or *I'll* put a bullet in you.'

140

For a couple of minutes, Handy explained his story, mainly what had happened up at the McGovren cabin, how Carter Krate and Broome's son, Felix, had died.

'Yeah, well, there was nobody in the cabin. Well no body, that is,' Joe quipped without humour. 'Only some well-roasted yearlin' meat.'

'You asked me why *I* didn't kill *you*,' Handy said, after a moment of tangled thoughts. 'Well, why didn't you kill Broome?' he asked, with an expression that held more than one reading.

'It don't say much for my judgement, I know, but I haven't wanted him dead since me an' Hector Chaf rode in,' Joe answered truthfully. 'Now, thinkin' on what happens if we run into any o' Broome's men, are you ridin' my way, or takin' the owlhoot trail?' he asked.

'While I'm still alive, I'll take my chances with you.'

'Yeah, me too.' As they rode, Joe was wondering on the whereabouts of Tark Jollife and his riders. He hoped they hadn't discovered the camp, or that they were now leading them there.

After another hour's ride, they were a few miles further south than Joe had thought. He looked about him for a landmark, soon made out the lone, darkly rising oak against the lightening sky.

Hector, Lunes and Gitano stood silent and vigilant in the brush as Joe and Duff Handy rode within twenty feet of them.

'I know you're there,' Joe said, without raising his voice. 'I've known it for most o' the night.'

'Yeah, so you should've,' Hector returned. 'Anyone else would o' got a blast from Ben's ol' scattergun.'

'It's good to be back, Hec.' The relief in Joe's voice was palpable. 'I went to visit Broome out at the ranch, an' brought back a keepsake. How's Ben? He is back here, ain't he?'

Hector smiled warmly. 'Yeah, he's back. He's goin' to spend the rest of his miserable life goin' gimp, but he'll trade that for seein' you safe. I think he feels bad about what happened out there.'

Megan appeared to gain no pleasure at Joe's safe return. As he entered the camp, she gave an uneasy, questioning nod towards Handy and moved away from her father.

'You're old enough to have won a limp,' Joe said moments later, as he knelt beside Ben. 'The rest o' you all right?'

'Who knows?' Ben said and lifted a hand towards Joe. 'Gitano says it'll take at least a couple o' years afore I can do much. He knows about these things.'

'Yeah, I just bet he does,' Joe responded and smiled caringly. Then he drew Hector off to one side. 'Does that sound like someone who's goin' to die?' he asked.

Hector shrugged thoughtfully. 'Gitano says he needs town doctorin'. His war bag don't contain much for the sepsis.'

'Then we'll get him out of here soon,' and Joe's words represented a promise.

'You know that Gitano an' Lunes ain't too pleased about you bringin' Handy in here. If he decides to run, none of us'll get out alive,' Hector said.

Joe shook his head. 'He won't run, Hec. He's the one who really ain't got nowhere to go, believe me. As for Broome, well we ain't goin' to fight him or his men in the open again.'

'We ain't? So what you got in mind, *jefe*?'

'It's a long-shot idea, but I reckon we can make it. You, me, Handy an' Gitano.'

Hector looked surprised. 'Four of us to take on

Broome?' he said. 'Have you seen Gitano mutterin' in fear, then crossin' himself every time he hears Broome's name mentioned?'

'Yep. I know. But he'll see the light after I have a talk with him.'

'An' how about Handy? Are you trustin' him?'

'Oh yeah,' Joe answered, and looked to where Handy was talking to Megan. 'Right now, our enemy's enemy really *is* our friend.'

For most of the remainder of the day, Joe couldn't help wondering why it was that Megan was so cool towards him. Eventually, he came to the conclusion that it was because he'd put her pa in danger, not because she was shy of any real feeling towards him. He'd spoken confidentially to Gitano. No one knew what it was that he'd said, but the man had agreed to go along with his plans. As Joe expected, Handy decided it was an opportune moment to tie in with them.

As the shadows lengthened, Hector, Gitano and Joe lay dozing. Quedo Lunes was closely watching Ben, tending to him every now and again with encouraging words and a trickle of his own Pass whiskey.

In the shadow of her small lodge, Megan again picked up a conversation with Duff Handy.

'So, where is it you're goin' tonight?' she asked casually, but with a shade of savvy.

'How do you know we're goin' anywhere?' Handy asked distrustfully.

Megan gave a sigh and smiled. 'Because that's the reason they're all taking forty-winks, except you o' course. It's obvious you're goin' somewhere.'

'I'm sayin' nothin', 'cause I know nothin' an' that's a fact,' Handy said.

'Well, if he is keepin' things that close, I can't say I blame him. There's a big of patch o' dirt at stake,' Megan responded. 'You might as well get your head down. I'll take over from Quedo.'

The men stood in a small group near the lone oak. They were waiting for full dark before leaving cover of the pear. Joe's face was set and grim, and it wasn't entirely due to their mission. But he wasn't going to say goodbye, not to Megan, Ben or Quedo Lunes. As far as he was concerned, it was just another way of saying something that he didn't mean.

'Well, let's go an' upset a few folk,' Hector said. Then they mounted their horses and Joe led them from the thicket.

26

Tark Jollife had recruited two men and ridden back to the thicket where they had laid up for Joe and Ben. They trawled the area thoroughly, found nothing except a thick crust of flies on a patch of dried blood.

'Yeah, this'll be about where we hit the other one,' Jollife said.

'Well, there ain't no sign of him now. Not even a well-picked bone,' one of his men answered back,

The third rider was looking around him with a clear distaste. 'Kind o' spooky here,' he remarked. 'There ain't nothin' livin' but us,'

'They're here all right, you just can't see 'em,' the other man replied.

'We're not bein' paid to get spooked by nothin',' Jollife said, but he too was taking an anxious look around.

'We can't spend *any* money if we're spread out here with a mob o' vultures stompin' all over our carcasses,' one of the other two suggested darkly.

'Yeah, there's somethin' that ain't square,' the other one said. 'There's a chill cuttin' through here, an' it ain't just the time o' year. I reckon Frog Petty had the right idea by drawin' pay. I'm headin' back. We'll think up somethin' to tell the boss.'

The trio turned and rode for the ranch. By and large

they were unimaginative, mercenary men, but now something had broken their morale, and Jollife cursed ineffectively.

'No sign . . . nothin',' Jollife reported to an increasingly troubled Broome. 'We're just wastin' your time an' money chasin' banshees.'

Broome glared silently for a moment before he spoke. 'So, what shall I do? Sit here twiddlin' thumbs, waitin' for old age to kill 'em off?'

'No, boss, me an' the boys been thinkin',' Jollife started by putting their contrived idea forward. 'Why not send for a party o' Rangers? Some of 'em ain't too chary o' visitin' this neck o' the woods if the dollars are right. They got a natural loathin' of rustlers an' the like, if that's who we're goin' after,' he added with a devious grin.

Broome threw Jollife a mean look. 'I got to think this through,' he said. 'I know the brush as well as any of 'em, so if needs be, I'll go out there myself. But if I do, there won't be any bonuses payable, you included.'

After full dark, Broome sat moodily in the big room that was his den. He looked around him, apprehensively, before pouring himself a large glass of whiskey. But he knew that most crimes along the Rio Bonito were committed in the open, not by loners who skulked through houses looking for open windows and unlocked doors.

The year had moved into November – only three more weeks until the peaceful possession title to the Standing K became lawful. But despite all his attempts to silence them, he knew in his bones that Joe Kettle, Ben McGovren and Hector Chaf had somehow regrouped. They weren't going to let any of it happen, least of all, the 'peaceful' bit. So somehow he'd have to keep them out in the brush, where they sought protection from him and his hired men. And if the young Kettle didn't make it to town before the last

146

Thursday of the month, Brent Perser would burn the filed counter-claim and the land would be his.

Over the years, Broome had built up many accounts in cattlemen's banks between El Paso and Albuquerque. The neighbouring territory and its peoples were growing up, becoming settled and civic minded. Within a very few years, the Standing K land would be worth a fortune, and that was all he wanted. He'd retain the cattle business as a blind, have to weed out those who knew too much.

Appeased by his own bigoted reckoning, but also worn down by the stress and the whiskey, Broome dozed in his big, wing-back chair. Shortly, he dreamed of Hector and Ben, the bad things that had happened between them. Hector was standing over him, leering. 'It's all right Wil, we ain't come to kill you. We got other stuff to do before that.' Hector was so close now that Broome could hear the man's tense intake of breath. Only Broome wasn't dreaming.

'This is most o' your nightmares come true,' Hector continued. 'But I'm keepin' one or two back, o' course.'

Broome's heart thumped, he cursed with shock and made an unthinking move forward.

Hector swiftly pushed the barrel of his Colt hard into the man's chest, cornered him back in his chair. 'You just stay there an' listen to what young Joe's got to say,' he said. 'An' yeah, in case you're still wonderin', he *really* is the son o' Jasper.'

Joe smiled casual. 'We're gettin' to be old friends, ain't we, Mr Broome?' Joe started off. 'You an' Hec can settle your personal differences later. All I want is what's mine, an' you're the only one who can give it me.'

'I'll see you in hell, kid,' Broome rasped.

'Maybe you will, Mr Broome, but it won't be just yet. Come in,' Joe then called out. 'Here's one o' the men you hired to kill my uncle,' Joe said flatly, as a moment later,

Gitano suspiciously entered the room, 'I thought you might recognize him,' he continued. 'Quedo Lunes knows the full story, an' I can produce him too, when the time comes. You remember him? Maybe his wife an' pretty daughter? They had an adobe just outside o' town.'

'What the hell is it you want?' Broome gasped, his mind trying to make sense of a desperate situation.

'Dumb question, even for a pants rat like you,' Joe snapped back. 'You're ridin' with me to Lemmon, an' you're signin' a quit claim deed. That'll be everythin' you say was deeded to you by Judd Kettle. That *was* goin' to be all,' he continued, 'but I changed my mind just recently. Now I want bank cheques for all the money you've got on deposit.'

'That's robbery. My money ain't yours,' Broome seethed back.

'I know,' Joe said and smiled icily.

'What happens to me then?' Broome asked.

'Couldn't care less. I'll probably turn you loose in the street, an' if there's anyone wants to shoot you dead, they can. There's no one comes to mind to stop 'em.'

'An' if I refuse to sign?'

'Ha, that's about as likely as the sun not risin' tomorrow,' Joe quipped back.

'I still got my men, Kettle, if that is your name,' Broome tried an implied threat.

'But not many, I'll wager. Once they know the trouble you're in, they won't fight. Why should they?' Joe responded and turned to Gitano. 'Go get a rope an' hog-tie him,' he said, then turned back to Broome. 'We don't want you leapin' out o' that chair an' escapin', do we?' he chuckled sarcastically.

'What about me?' Handy asked of Joe. 'Do I figure in all this?' he asked anxiously.

148

'Yeah, you do,' Joe said. 'When Gitano's finished, you an' him go hire a single rig an' ride back to the camp. Bring everyone in, an' if we ain't here, just wait. We will be back, understand?'

'Yes, boss,' Handy said, and attempted what he thought was an honest smile.

Joe caught sight of Hector's face, flinched when he saw the suppressed, murderous look in his eyes. He was going to ask Hector to watch Broome while he went to the main door of the ranch house, but then didn't bother. 'Back in a moment,' he said, instead.

At the front of the house he opened the door a foot or so and took a look across the yard towards the corrals and the 'punchers' bunkhouse. 'Jollife, get yourself over here,' he yelled, waited a moment then loudly called the man's name again. Then he pushed the door to and returned to the den.

When Tark Jollife arrived and edged his way through the door, he stopped and stared. He had never seen Hector before, but he remembered that Joe was the man they had roped and captured and brought in from the pear thickets. He noted their guns, that Broome was now the one under duress.

'Time's run out, I'm afraid, Tarky,' Broom started.

'Last bit's true enough,' Hector echoed, as Broome continued.

'I'm sellin' everythin' to the Kettles. It's sort o' dust to dust. But it means that you an' whoever's left on the payroll's got to draw pay. As foreman you got authority, so ride to Lemmon an' get it done, will you?'

Jollife had a careful look around him then backed from the room. He'd seen and heard enough to know there was something wrong, but knew better than to hang around or ask questions. As he stood on the veranda looking towards the bunkhouse and the few men that were left, 'chickens come home to roost' was the instant and obvious expression that came to mind. He cursed Broome, the Kettles and his own luck. Riding away was no problem, suited him just fine. It had been obvious from what Max Pepper had to say that men wouldn't follow Broome again. He didn't know exactly what had holed the Broome boat, and he didn't care. He smiled when he suddenly realized he was boss-simple no more, that he'd also gained authority to pay himself an owed bonus.

An hour later, Joe and Hector were standing either side of Broome as they walked across the yard. They'd waited until the men had cleared the home pasture and crossed the Rio Bonito.

'What now?' Broome asked impassively.

'We get *our* horses an' we ride. You pick yourself a clear-foot with a big ass on it, 'cause you'll need it,' Hector advised him, with more stern emotion.

Another fifteen minutes, and the three of them used the same river crossing. But unlike Jollife and the others, they took the trail for Lemmon. Hector remained grim, couldn't lose the thought of a final retribution with Broome.

Ben McGovren had been moved to the lodge, and now he was sleeping soundly on Megan's cot. When his own Pass whiskey had run dry, he'd been won over by the warm mescal that Quedo Lunes had liberally administered. In the early hours, Lunes insisted that Megan also took some sleep while he looked to her pa. Worn out from just about every-thing, she buckled onto a blanket, without even removing her boots. The question of where the four riders had gone and what they were doing was in her mind for almost a minute before she fell into a deep sleep.

It was the slivers of rising sunlight through the east-facing side of the lodge that woke her. Lunes who was crouched in the doorway, but still watching Ben, put his fingers to his lips for her to remain quiet.

She looked and saw Ben's chest rise and fall with slow, regular breathing. 'Why? He's OK isn't he?' she asked.

'Oh yes, Megan, he's OK . . . just less trouble when he's asleep. Like goats, they too sleep when they're not well.'

Megan smiled tiredly. 'Well, he has been called that before,' she muttered. She stepped from the lodge to be confronted by Duff Handy and Gitano. The two men had returned to the camp very soon after she fell asleep.

She stared at the rig, noticed its shiny panels were scored and scraped where it had been driven through the scrub.

'Where's Hector and Joe?' she asked them.

'Where they should be, guess,' Handy replied.

'Just tell me where they are,' she said, her throat dry and constricted.

'Sorry, I meant they were at the Standin' K ranch house,' Handy explained.

'Sufferin' cabin fever with Broome an' his hired killers?' she enquired testily.

'Not exactly. The killers ain't killin' any longer, an' they ain't hired either. Joe an' Hector's got Broome there on his own, Megan. It looks like the trouble's just about over.'

'I'm tired o' what things look like,' she said, and was beginning to show it.

Gitano nodded at Megan. 'It's different this time,' he agreed. 'The rig's for Ben, an' it was Joe sent us to get you. We're to get back there pronto . . . all of us.'

'All right.' Megan raised her hands in acceptance. 'Let's get goin' before somethin' makes it not so different,' she said.

There was no sign of life at the Standing K, except the bunkhouse dog and its friend. They carried Ben into the empty house and made him comfortable on the sofa under the high-beamed ceiling of the den. Megan sat beside him and Lunes looked around for Broome's whiskey. Handy went with Gitano to unsaddle the horses before turning them loose in the corral. They searched the rest of the ranch buildings, bunkhouse and outhouses, but saw no one. It was as Joe said it might be.

'It looks like they *have* gone,' Gitano said, finally lowering the barrel of his rifle.

'They'll be makin' for Lizard Pass, trailin' Max Pepper's prints all the way to Colorado, if they got any sense,' Handy replied, having finally got his nerves under control.

'I wonder why the dogs never went with 'em,' Gitano said with uncaring surprise. 'I'm cold, let's get back in the house, an' I'll light us a big fire.'

27

It was pushing midday when three horsemen dismounted in front of the town hall at Lemmon. When they stepped up to the front door of the building, Joe was close beside Broome, and Hector was a pace behind. As well as a few townsfolk who saw them, Lawyer Daggert was watching from the window of his office. He told himself that, if they were wanting his particular services they'd have to ask, because he wasn't about to offer. He'd already spoken to Tark Jollife, advised him and the rest of Broome's men to clear the town after drawing their pay. 'That's good advice, an' it's for free,' he'd said.

As a consequence, Jollife and his cohorts were long gone when the riders came to town. Daggert watched them until they had entered the town hall building, then he sat down and thoughtfully considered his part in the consequences.

Broome wasted no time once they were in the clerk's office. 'Get out your records, Perser,' he commanded. 'Look up the quitclaim deed to the Standin' K. You know the one, the one that's from Judd Kettle to me. I want you to write one just like it from me to Kettle.'

'Bruno Joseph Kettle,' Joe bluntly advised.

Neither Joe nor Hector spoke while the clerk was writing the deed. When it was finished, Broome signed it and had his signature acknowledged.

153

'File that for record, an' withdraw the suit that's already there,' Joe said as he paid the fees. Then he indicated that he, Broome and Hector leave the office. 'Let's get shot o' this place,' he said with displeasure.

Out on the walkway, Joe turned suddenly to Broome. 'Well, now I know what I've got, mister,' he started to say. 'There's the house an' the land, an' a whole load o' prime livestock to go with it. You,' he continued, 'you got nothin' except the horse I'm lettin' you keep.'

Broome took a hesitant step away, as if he wasn't sure what Joe was going to do or say next.

Joe smiled coldly. 'I don't know what the court's goin' to decide, but if I was you, I'd think on all the places not to go within ten miles of, before ridin' the hell out o' here,' he threatened.

Hector laughed. 'The boy's all heart,' he put in, with a smirk even chillier than Joe's. 'You know I ain't quite so accommodatin'.'

Broome now felt the grip of revenge, as his old adversary confronted him, the sudden free-running sweat between his shoulder blades. 'What are you goin' to do with me?' he demanded.

'Takin' you out a ways to make sure you cross the Rio Bonito. I'm makin' sure you don't ever think o' returnin'.'

'You mean, makin' sure I can't,' Broome sneered.

'Just get on your horse an' ride south,' Hector commanded. 'Me an' Joe's goin' to be right with you, but I'll tell you when to rein in. Get goin', he rasped.

The three men rode for nearly an hour. It was to where a stand of oaks met a ford of the Rio Bonito. It was also where Broome had planned the rustling of Standing K cattle, so many years before.

'You recognize this place?' Hector called out. 'Get down, an' take a look around.'

Broome cast a wary look around him, waited with bleak anticipation as Hector and Joe rode close.

'You're a murderin', thievin' piece o' scum, Broome, an' I've been at fault for not shootin' you years ago,' Hector said as he dismounted. Without taking his eyes off Broome, he unbuckled his gunbelt and handed it up to Joe who remained sitting his horse with quiet interest. Then he moved forward purposefully, cursed under his breath with the frustration of wanting it all over.

Broome threw out his chin. 'You know, Chaf, I reckon you just ain't got the guts to shoot me,' he sneered.

Hardly a muscle moved in Hector's face, as he retaliated, He lashed out very quickly with his right fist and Broome's head went back like the hinge on a cow pen. The man's lips were splitting tight against his jaw of rot-coloured teeth, and when his shoulders, backside and heels hit the ground flat out, Hector was on him.

Broome was badly shaken, but his extraordinary instinct for survival was still working. He half turned, flung an arm around Hector's neck, and clung tight. Hector's knuckles drove into the back of the man's big head, but Broome swung himself over. Face down, he rose to get onto all-fours, and with brute strength, reached for another neck grip.

Hector dodged him and threw all his weight forward. Broome collapsed into the attack and together they rolled through the patches of cheat, snarling and growling with fury. They were struggling for an advantage, clawing for each other as ferocious as a pair of grizzlies.

They managed to climb to their feet, stood toe to toe, shocking each other with their enraged punches. Blood was oozing from their mouths and noses as Broome snapped them into a clinch. They staggered from side to side, backwards and forwards before going down heavily, with Hector underneath. Broome thrust his left forearm under Hector's chin and with the fingers of his right hand gouged at his eyes. Hector lifted a leg as high as he could with his heel against Broome. He kicked inward and thrust his boot back down sharply. With a bellow of pain, Broome flung himself away, staggered to regain his balance. One leg of his pants had been ripped open, and blood streamed from where Hector's prick spur had torn its way through.

They quartered the ground as they fought, sometimes throwing punches, sometimes manoeuvring for a hand-hold. Their lungs began to labour and rasp, and they staggered in unbalanced circles. Eventually, the muscles in their arms lost control, and their legs dragged heavily.

Broome was the heavier, stronger man, but he lacked the thoughtful purpose of Hector. Watching cautiously, Hector knew that if the fight went on much longer, they'd both go down. They were too old for anything else, and the one who went down fast, would stay there longest.

Broome was slumping now, could hardly lift his fists. He fought only in futile, defensive spurts and, as if to prove it, he lowered his head and went forward in one last despairing attack. A lucky aimless blow flung Hector across the bowl of one of the oaks, and thrashing even more wildly Broome plunged forward to try and finish the fight.

But Hector was still thinking and he ducked, twisting quickly to one side. Broome missed with his punch and rolled hard around the meat of the tree. Hector grunted, eased himself back and settled for grabbing as much of Broome's hair and ears as he could. He drew the man's head back and with the years of frustration and antagonism welling up, he smashed his face just once solidly against the ridges of crusty bark.

Broome's thick-set body gave out and he sank to the ground, his head falling to the shallow water that curled close around the roots of the oak. Breathless, Hector lost his balance, and he fell exhausted on top of Broome. For a short time, both men lay without stirring, then Hector pushed himself away. But he stopped when he noticed the man's shattered face was under the water, crushing against the river-bed. He gripped the dark coat around the man's shoulders, and exerting his remaining strength, dragged Broome's upper body clear of the water.

Taking support from the tree, Hector looked down at the swollen, bruised face of the man he'd wanted to fight, the man he'd wanted to kill only minutes earlier. But he was too weary for any sentiment and, regaining his footing, he wiped his face with his wet hands and painfully limped away. 'Once upon a time, *he* wanted to kick the bejasus out o' *me*,' he said to no one.

Hector glanced up at Joe, held out his hand and took his gunbelt back. He drew the big bone-handled .44 Colt from its holster, and drew back the hammer. Then he turned slowly, deliberately took aim and fired. The sound of the single shot crashed out, reverberated along the winding course of the river.

'In hell's name, why not?' Hector muttered and raised his eyes to Joe, as if there might be an answer there. 'That was for Quedo Lunes, Jasper Kettle an' Ben,' he said. 'I couldn't just let him ride away. The son-of-a-bitch would've known that.'

Joe nodded his understanding and grunted out a fitting noise. 'An' I'm takin' a horse back,' he said.

Hector buckled up his belt, reached deep into his pants pocket and walked back to where Broome lay dead. He kneeled beside the body and pressed his poke of ear bits into the clutch of the dead man's hand. 'Here,' he said, 'this'll pay the goddamn ferryman.'

'Do you reckon there's any o' Broome's men left? Do you reckon they could be out here, layin' for us?' Joe asked minutes later as they turned towards the Standing K.

'If there are, I'll leave 'em for you, son,' Hector replied. 'I'm driftin' into a short saddle nap.'

'Where's Broome?' Quedo Lunes asked immediately Hector and Joe returned.

'Gone to his last roundup. So he won't be passin' for a long while,' Hector told him.

'Where's Megan? How's Ben?' Joe asked in nervous, quick succession.

Lunes started to say that Ben was up and about. He pointed towards the house, but Joe and Hector were already headed that way. They went straight to the den and sat down. There was a fire and they waited for the chill to ease from their bones.

'Just leave 'em be, Joe. They're turnin' in, doin' what all sensible God-fearin' folk should be doin',' Hector advised tiredly. 'There's plenty o' time for all that we got to tell 'em.'

So Joe closed his eyes, but he didn't go to sleep straight away. He spent an hour mulling on plans for their futures, some new beginnings. He tried to place Megan in his thoughts, but there was something missing. Perhaps it was what he'd seen between her and Duff Handy, whatever that was. The main thing was, he'd got back the ranch and most of its stock. That's what he owed his pa, and the Kettles before that.

Weeks passed and Gitano was now working with the new hands they'd hired. Now and again he'd go missing, and Quedo Lunes said he'd go back to the lodge camp hidden deep in the wildness of the pear and mesquite. Quedo himself had regained a lot of his former character. He spent most of his time looking over stock, would sit outside of the bunkhouse in the long evenings, jawing with Joe Kettle's 'punchers. Duff Handy eventually drew pay, said he'd ride up to Flora Vista to find work. Joe wasn't that disappointed or troubled by the move. He guessed the man would try and team up with some of his old associates at the stockyards.

One day when they had taken the wagon to town for stores, Joe asked Ben about the relationship between Hector and Broome. 'It must've been somethin' real bad to smoulder away for so many years,' he said.

'I ain't sure, Joe, but I always thought it was somethin' to do with Quedo's daughter, Clemente,' Ben confided. 'Somethin' happened after her death, but Hec weren't one for lettin' on. He put his feelin's into a very dark room, together with those he held for Broome. He locked the door, but never threw away the key. He was always goin' to come back an' open up.'

'Well, I reckon he sure has now,' Joe said. 'An' there's a new life here that he can busy himself with.'

'I can't see *me* gettin' much of a new life,' Ben rumbled.

'How'd you mean, Ben?'

'First, we ain't got a home any more. Second, I probably lost my daughter, an' third, I got some real awkward wifely business in Lemmon that needs attendin' to.'

'Hey, wait up there, feller,' Joe said. 'My gran'pa, an' his pa before him, gave your pa deed to a section. I know it was one o' them dollar nominal sections, but the sentiment was bindin' an' for keeps. That ain't ever goin' to change,' he offered.

'It already has. All that's left is a heap o' goddamn ashes.'

'Only the cabin. We build you a *bigger an' better* one, like I promised. That's your home, an' that's where you'll stay. Besides, I reckon *whatever* that problem is you got in Lemmon, you'd be a darn more persuasive with a new home backin' you up,' Joe added with a wry smile. 'We'll even raise a fence with a latch gate. What do you say?'

'Yeah, it could work,' Ben said slowly, and with an expressive grin. 'An' I still got some saddle-brokes up at the Muleshoe tank. With a bit o' help, I *could* start over.'

'Hah, you're damn right you could,' Joe agreed. 'Now I'd like to have a word with that daughter o' yours,' he said.

Megan was standing beside the corral. With a small fruit knife, she was pensively carving notches into the top rail.

'It looks like we got most folk on the Standin' K sorted out, Megan,' Joe began. 'O' course, you got your own life, an' what you do with it's up to you. I was wonderin' if you had anythin' particular in mind,' he proposed with a fairly cheerless uncertainty.

'I reckon I'll be stayin' with Pa,' she answered after a moment. 'There *was* once a man I had feelin's an' a particular mind for, but he never noticed me, if *that's* what you're wonderin'.'

'Ah, I reckon I know who you're talkin' about,' Joe said. 'An' believe me, if he hadn't have had other stuff on his mind, that feller woulda done a darn sight more'n notice you,' he suggested, sensing the drift of encouragement.

Megan carved an extra large wedge from the corral rail. 'So, you reckon you know this man I'm talkin' about?' she queried with a slight, dry smile.

'Well, if he's who I'm thinkin' of, I hear he's steadfast, hard-workin' an' wealthy ... well-featured, too. You'd do well to let him know you're still interested, Megan.'

'Oh, I intend to, Joe,' Megan said, and this time they exchanged mutual, more significant smiles.